JENNERCIDE

by

Mike Scantlebury

"Mickey from Manchester: Book 11"

CHAPTER ONE: Poison on a plate

"Why here?" Mickey said irritably.

"We had to meet somewhere," Dr Jenner said. "Somewhere public, central, near the centre of Manchester. Easily accessible by bus and train, public transport. And I wasn't going to go to your office, or your house. Sorry. I have to take precautions."

No, I mean why *here*, Mickey was thinking. It wasn't the place agreed.

The Doctor had made a great fuss about the need he said to select a suitable venue, then invited Mickey to suggest a place. Mickey said Essy's Cafe, as it was a favourite haunt of his, and the man concurred. Then, when Mickey came walking up the street, he found Jenner waiting outside. He took Mickey's elbow and hustled him around the corner into another cafe, a dive called 'Miles'. A place, he later confirmed, that neither man had been to before. Ever.

"We talked on the phone," the Doctor said, his voice low and breathless as they walked.

That explained everything? Mickey didn't think so!

They talked, right. So that would mean someone would have to be listening in, if they were going to find out the planned rendezvous. Jenner's phone was bugged? Mickey was pretty sure his wasn't. After all, he had access to Terry at Regional Office. That man could make a brick talk. Or, if need be, he could encrypt a tabloid newspaper. He was good at such things.

"You're being overly cautious," Mickey suggested.

The Doctor didn't seem to think so. He said that he had evidence that his voice and e-mail were bugged. Well, Mickey couldn't wait. He wanted to see something definite. So far, this man had given him nothing.

It wasn't even a job!

Not that Mickey had a job at the moment, a 'proper' job. He'd given many years service in the defence of his country, but he was signed out and paid off, given a pension and a few discrete medals. Still, nobody ever retired from the Secret Service. Captain Gibson, his boss of many years, said that Mickey was 'on retainer'. That was the polite way of saying it.

Still, that meant assignments came and went, and Mickey reported for duty when ordered. In between, he was on his own.

Like now. This week he had been planning spending time with a paintbrush and some wallpaper, sprucing up his new house in North Salford. Then he got the mysterious telephone call. Dr Jenner introduced himself and said he was a 'friend of a friend'. He said that Mickey had been 'recommended'. He needed some help, evidently, and thought Mickey could oblige.

Who had given him that idea? Mickey

wondered, irritated again. The Doctor was being so secretive. He had said nothing definite, about that or any other details. He wanted to meet in person, he was insistent on that.

It would all be explained then, he assured Mickey.

Mickey should have made some excuse, he began thinking, immediately after. Still, he was intrigued. He had asked around at the office, and, surprise, surprise, Terry had heard of the man. He said he was 'Nobel Prize material'. An important researcher, with a reputation in the field of biotechnology. Terry had seen his articles on the internet. Jenner had written books.

Mickey took a seat in the corner of the cafe, away from the door, and accepted the offer of a frothy coffee. He sat and waited for the man to fetch it, and looked around. No one suspicious. No spies. No men in rain coats, glancing their way.

A quiet day in Manchester.

Mickey looked at Dr Jenner, as he struggled to find cash and pay for the goods. Typical absent-minded Professor. He had straggling hair, grey and unkempt. His suit was expensive, but worn, with stains along the lapels and under the pockets. He looked as though he slept in it. The man's skin was sallow, worn, as if he had spent time travelling in the Tropics.

Mickey sighed. What was he thinking of, agreeing to meet? It wouldn't end well.

It was nearly mid-day.

"I've taken the liberty of ordering you a sandwich," Jenner said quietly, as he sat down.

Mickey stared. He was hungry?

Mickey didn't usually bother about such things. He ate when he was hungry. Years of being away from home, working odd hours, staying up late, he didn't bother with the niceties. He was touched. The man was trying to be thoughtful.

"Do you have any recording devices on your person?" Dr Jenner said, as if it was his usual conversation opener.

Mickey made a point of emptying his pockets. No, he said. This won't be recorded.

At least, he was thinking, until I've heard anything that is worth saving. I've heard nothing yet.

Jenner said: "You look like a policeman."

Mickey shrugged. He had heard that. He was a big man, wide at the shoulders. People generally assumed he was some kind of mature sportsman, maybe someone who had left the sport of his choice and was now earning wages representing sporting goods companies, or commentating on the radio. He had a big smile when he found it. He was good with people, usually.

This wasn't one of those days.

Mickey decided to come straight to the point.

"Who put you on to me?" he asked the Doctor.

It had to be someone who had Mickey's private number, his home phone. Maybe a colleague.

"Dolf."

Mickey stared. Then he took a breath. Then he counted to ten.

Dolf wasn't a colleague. Not any more. He had been sacked by Captain Gibson when the boss found out that Dolf had been selling secrets, betraying his country. In the old days, Dolf might have faced a firing squad.

"He's no friend of mine," Mickey said, struggling to keep calm.

"Strange. He said you were quite close."

Once. Maybe. They had worked together, during the election, the last General Election. It hadn't ended well.

"Sandwiches, gentlemen," a voice said.

Looking up, Mickey saw an older man standing over them, a plate in either hand. He was dressed in black and white.

"This, I think, is for you," he said to Jenner, proffering the plate. The Doctor nodded, so the chef put the other plate in front of Mickey and left, walking away, not looking back. He didn't seem interested in them, once the food had been supplied.

"What have you got?" Mickey asked, not really interested.

Jenner looked at Mickey, quietly, as if weighing him up. There was a pause.

Then he said, at last: "Do you mind if we

swap?"

Mickey stared again. This is getting wierder, he was thinking.

He lifted the nearest slab of white bread on his sandwich, suddenly keen to see what he might be losing. It was cheese and pickle. A favourite. How did the scientist know that? It couldn't be Dolf. Mickey had only started on cheese a few months ago, when Melia told him he was eating too much meat. She cared about him, she said. She didn't want him to face an early death.

"What have you got?" Mickey asked the older man again.

"Tongue."

Mickey scowled. It might be a Northern delicacy, he was thinking, but he had never liked it.

"Let's get this straight," he said quietly. "You've never been in this place before, you say, and yet you think it's possible that the staff might have tried to poison your lunch. Your answer is to swap platters. That way, if they want to kill one of us, it ends up being me. You don't mind that? But you want my help in defending yourself against your enemies, somehow. Is that it?"

The researcher, having achieved the exchange, started biting at the cheese sandwich. He was chewing, but he nodded.

"You seriously think you're in danger?"

The Doctor put down the half-eaten morsel. "I know they're trying to poison me," he said.

Mickey had no reply to that. He took a bite. The meat wasn't half bad, or, at least, not as bad as he was expecting.

"What's in your water?" the scientist asked.

Mickey was taken aback. He looked at the table. He had been given a coffee, as asked for, and they had served him with a glass of water too. He looked around. That was common in Mediterranean countries. Was this cafe foreign?

"Tap water," Mickey said, guessing. "No worries. It's been filtered." He had no doubt about that.

Jenner nodded. "It might have gone through a carbon filter, to kill bacteria. It might have been dripped through sand, to removed larger particulates. It might even have endured ultra-violet light, U.V., too. This is Manchester, and one thing you can say about the area is that it's one of the few places in the country that doesn't add fluoride, so we know that. Also, this city gets water piped in from the Lake District, so it's hard water, less calcium than down south."

So? That all sounded good. Mickey wasn't being put off drinking it.

"You have a girlfriend?" the Doctor asked.

Mickey nodded. Melia. He had a relationship with Amelia Hartliss, a peer in the anti-terrorism unit that was WSB.

Jenner asked: "Is she taking birth control pills?"

Mickey chewed on his sandwich. Good question. He was the old-fashioned type, so it wasn't a subject he was happy to discuss with his lady. Still, he presumed she was. She was on the cusp of thirty, so, still young enough to have children.

He nodded. The Doctor smiled.

"The pills are full of hormones, female hormones like oestrogen," he told the sometime security agent. "She pees it out, it goes into the drain and that water is recycled and pumped back into the city's taps. They can't get the hormones out of the water. Or antibiotics that are fed to dairy cattle. Or run-off from farms, stuff like phosphates and nitrates. Additives."

Mickey raised a hand. Stop! Stop! He got the picture. He didn't think he would get the image out of his mind.

"You don't have that problem," he sneered.

Jenner looked down. He had a bottle of water in front of him. A bottle, Mickey noted. Was that safe?

"This water comes from Somerset," he said. He had brought it with him. It was the only stuff he would drink, he said. "The water is filtered through the limestone levels of the Mendip Hills. It takes a while to get through. The water in this bottle could be a thousand years old, old enough to miss out on all of the modern contaminants. Yes, it's safe."

"I know you."

Mickey looked up. A new figure had arrived, even more haggard and bedraggled than Jenner, with a wispy beard. He was staring at the two men, and his eyes were wild and dilated. He looked quite mad. He looked ready to attack.

Dr Jenner gasped, pushed back his chair against the wall and looked about to flee, but he couldn't: his path was blocked.

He was spooked, panicking. He grabbed at his cutlery, brushing the plates aside, as if looking for a weapon.

Oh great, Mickey was thinking. He's going to stab this tramp with a fork.

Mickey sighed, wondering what he was going to do next.

* * * * *

At the same time, Melia was in another cafe in central Manchester, about half a mile away.

She was meeting her cousin Liv.

"I don't like the look of this," Melia was saying, poking at the burger on her plate. "I don't know, I've had no appetite recently. I don't fancy any of my usuals. I still like curry, but I'm having trouble keeping it down."

She looked at the bun Liv was holding up to her mouth.

"You want that gherkin?" Melia asked suddenly.

Liv dropped it onto Melia's plate and she wolfed it down, licking her lips after.

"I must be getting old," she observed. "I only like strong flavours."

Liv sighed. Your taste in food, she was thinking, matches your taste in men, cousin.

"Sorry," Melia said, wiping her mouth.

"You've got a new relationship - You've met somebody new?"

No, not new, Liv was thinking. But she couldn't say that: Melia knew the person she was seeing. Maybe that was why she couldn't say the name, not now. Maybe later, when she could see that it was going to last.

Melia had skirted around the subject. Ever since she had found out her cousin was gay, she'd been reluctant to discuss 'friends' with her. It was a shame. When they were younger, and went out together, into town, chasing men, they had so much in common, so much to talk about. Now, not so much. Melia had no idea what she should say, or could say.

Melia looked at her cousin. She was tall, like her, blonde hair not auburn like Melia, but strong features, pretty when up close. When they were out on the prowl, they realised they presented a devastating package. They were strong women, and knew their own minds. They had their pick of suitors, rejected the tough artists and played the field, for many years.

Then Melia met Mickey and her whole world turned upside down. Liv was still keen to keep romancing, but Melia was suddenly preoccupied and didn't want to stalk the nightclubs with her cousin. Liv was disappointed, especially as she could see the new relationship wasn't at all good for Mel. The problem was that Mickey was hardly ever there. He was off - travelling the world, zapping the bad guys, spying for his country. He made one hell of an unreliable boyfriend.

Melia knew it, but she'd never admit it. She was besotted from the beginning. She never got serious about anybody else who strayed into her lifeafter that. She was hopelessly devoted to the man she called her 'soul mate'. She couldn't live without him.

But she didn't get much chance to live with him, either. Mickey, being Mickey, wasn't really there for her.

"Yeah," Liv admitted. "I've got a new partner. It's going really well, but I'll tell you if anything serious develops."

Like living together. The last woman who moved into Liv's house in Swinton ended up getting herself killed. Liv was wiped out by that, for months. That's why she was taking it slow now. She couldn't face another such blow to her fragile emotions.

"How's work?" Liv asked flippantly, not expecting an answer. You don't ask a spy what happens in the office.

Melia sighed and sipped at her lemon tea. There wasn't much to report, even if she'd been allowed to. Not since the European Referendum. That had thrown the whole country into turmoil. The dice were up in the air, nobody was sure where they'd land.

"Actually, I can tell you something," Melia admitted. "You remember Farmer MacLawn?"

On a previous mission, Melia had been

delegated to infiltrate the anti-fracking camp on Barton Moss. The tents and vans had been established right next to a farm owned by a handsome young man called MacLawn. He had taken a shine to Melia, but she let that slide. Then, recently, he had phoned her up, out of the blue. He said he had a 'problem'. He needed her help.

"Aren't they coming back?" Liv asked, finishing her meal.

Melia nodded. That was right. The new government had decided that fracking wasn't such a bad option, and they had approved developments in Lancashire. South of those projects, right here in Salford, the area of Barton Moss had been earmarked for future exploitation. The previous intrusion had only been for exploratory drilling. The expectation was that real work could start there, once planning permission had been granted. Melia doubted that Salford Council would want to say 'yes', but the national government could over-rule them. Yes, that was probably what the farmer wanted. It didn't thrill Melia to think about it. But what could she do?

Her phone rang. It was right there in front of her on the table. She looked at the display.

Liv said: "Yay, that farmer is keen. You gonna answer that?"

"Oh, I can call him back later," Melia said, off-hand. She smiled, and put her phone in her jacket pocket.

It was deception. She didn't want to admit the truth, even to her cousin. The call wasn't from her farmer friend, it was from Terry, in the office. He had been calling her a lot in the last few weeks. She didn't want to speak to him. She was putting it off.

"That burger wasn't enough," Liv announced. "I'm going for something extra, maybe an apple pie. You want one?"

Melia found herself gagging at the thought. Apple? Pastry? It made her feel sick to her stomach.

She waved her hand. "Good Luck with that," she said sarcastically. "They call it 'Fast Food', but it has to be the slowest service in the whole of Salford. I don't know why. Maybe they can't get the staff."

"They can't," Liv agreed. "The Manager told me about it, the last time I was here. They keep getting held up. Men with guns, apparently. It frightens off the workers. Good job you're here, Mel," she added sarcastically. "You're a Special Agent. You could handle them."

She stood up, turned, then froze in her tracks. She let out a little cry, almost a whimper.

Two men with ski masks had just come in the door and were heading determinedly towards the counter.

"On the floor!" one man screamed. He had a local accent. "Get down, everyone. All of you, hit the floor!"

Liv dropped to her knees, one side of the

table. She put her head down, trying not to be noticed.

One of the robbers noticed Melia.

He would have to be blind not to notice her. She was easily the best looking woman in the place. Long hair, well turned out. She was wearing a tight sweater that accented her natural curves. She was tall, lithe. A young man's dream.

This particular young man in question swaggered over, waving his pistol in a manner he'd learned from television.

"Maybe you didn't hear me," he said, his voice as low as he could force it.

Melia looked up and gave him an insolent look. She wasn't about to be frightened by amateurs.

"Oh, I heard you," she said brightly. "I just don't regularly take orders from pimply-faced little rats."

Also, she felt awful, her stomach churning. She thought she might need the toilet any moment. She didn't feel able to prostrate herself at that particular point in time. It might prove awkward, later.

The kid, anxious to impress, moved round to her side of the table and practically waved the gun in her face.

"I give the orders," he declared. "This gun gives the orders. You do what I say."

"Make your mind up," Melia told him. "Which is it?"

His squinty little eyes bulged behind the

mask. That was the only part of his ugly face that Melia could see, and she wasn't impressed by that. She could see anger in his gaze, but no confidence. Sure enough, he looked to his mate for help.

"What the hell you doing?" the other robber shouted. He had the cash till open and was helping himself. All around, people cowered. It was going well, he was thinking. What was his younger assistant up to, wasting his time on that woman?

Melia saw that the young man beside her was looking around. This is almost too easy, she thought, leaned over and closed her fingers on the gun. She twisted the guy's wrists, intending to loose off a bullet at his distant companion.

There was no shot.

"You've left the safety catch on!" Melia spluttered, staggered at his inefficiency.

She wrenched the pistol out of the kid's hands. It spun him round and he practically fell on top of her. Then righted himself, and stood up, resentfully. This crazy bitch was making a fool out of him. He raised a hand to her.

Melia grabbed his hand and turned him so that he was facing his partner and she was behind him. She knew what was going to happen. Sure enough, the more experienced criminal tried shooting at her, but the bullet went into his mate. Melia was protected by the body, and was able to level the gun under the kid's armpit and fire back. The man at the counter fell.

"You've done it!" Liv said, congratulating. "I knew you wouldn't let them get away with it, Mel."

Melia kicked the limp figure of the wounded kid out of her lap and started running for the toilet. She was suddenly overwhelmed with nausea, and her head was throbbing. She staggered across the floor and through the small door, Liv in pursuit.

She was ashamed of herself. She had been in plenty of gun fights. Nothing had ever made her sick before. Not like this.

As Melia hung over the toilet bowl, her cousin Liv moved in to grab her hair and pull it out of the way.

"Oh, Melia," she said. "How exciting. There's no doubt now, is there? You're pregnant!"

* * * * *

"It's my family that I really worry about," Jenner was saying.

Mickey was bored. He wasn't even sure if he liked this man, and yet he was being asked to protect him.

From what? He thought he was being listened in to; followed; threatened; poisoned. Well, maybe he was paranoid. When the homeless man came into the cafe and said, 'I know you', the Doctor assumed the wild character was talking to him. He wasn't. The guy was somebody that Mickey had once arrested, many years ago, and although he had an intimidating demeanour, all he really wanted was the price of a cup of coffee. Mickey gave him coins and he left, with a 'Thank You'.

Maybe Jenner was wrong about other things, Mickey was thinking. Maybe it wasn't as bad as he imagined.

The Doctor pulled a piece of paper out of his pocket and spread it on the table top, moving the coffee cup out of the way.

"I can't trust banks," he told Mickey. "If they can bug my phone, they can hack my bank account. So I've taken money out, over time, turned it into re-saleable items and buried it here," he said, pointing a finger.

A Treasure Map! Mickey was ready to believe anything now. This guy was off the wall, and off his head. Clearly.

"This is the first item of business," he said. "I want you to keep this map, Mickey. Keep it safe. If anything happens to me, my family will be taken care of. That gives me great peace of mind."

"Also this, Mickey," he added, reaching into an inner pocket and bringing a computer's memory stick out. He laid it on top of the map.

"This is my research," he said. "Most of it. There's documents, memos, records of meetings. It all needs hiding."

Mickey turned the USB pen over in his hand. It had a large capacity. There could be hundreds of documents on it.

"What will I find?" he asked quietly, wanting to be convinced.

"All about me."

"I don't know you."

"My name is Jenner. I've spent a lifetime researching foodstuffs. I'm the man who invented Sucrosanct, the most widely used sweetener in the industry. That sandwich you were eating? The bread has sweetener in it. The coffee? Sweetener added before it went in the jar. All 'sugary' drinks, all colas and lemonades. That's me. I led the team and we made a product that is slowly poisoning the world. I've tried to set the record straight but my employers want to shut me up. Permanently."

Mickey was chewing it over. This 'scientist' was pretty grandiose. He seemed to think he was important, all right, maybe capable of winning a Nobel Prize. He seemed to think he had a finger in all the pies. Everywhere.

"I'm not sure," Mickey started. "I don't really know what I could do for you. I don't know what Dolf was suggesting - "

"That you could keep me safe!"

Mickey shook his head. If this was a WSB job, they'd take the delightful Mr Jenner to a Safe House, and put in a team to watch him round the clock. It would be, maybe, nine operatives. Mickey couldn't do that sort of thing alone.

"Even if I stayed with you twenty four hours - " he said.

The Doctor cut him off. "I don't want to hear 'No'," he said bluntly. "Look, I've given you some important items. Keep them, at least. Keep them and think about it. I'll call you in a couple of days, and you can give me an answer then."

The truth was, Mickey realised, that this wasn't an assignment. If Captain Gibson had said to him, 'Look after this man, he's in danger', then he would be taking the whole project seriously. As it was, it just seemed like the ramblings of a confused and paranoid soul, too puffed up with his own importance. The world was out to get him? Of course it was!

They stood up and made their way towards the door. Nobody looked up. There was no pair of eyes following their progress. Where were these dangerous criminals, out to silence the whistle blower from the food industry?

Standing on the pavement, Mickey reached out to shake the man's hand, smile wryly and agree they would be in touch. He didn't see the car coming, but it hummed towards them, mounted the kerb and swept the scientist off his feet.

The bonnet of the car was a foot away from Mickey's legs. He saw a number of spotlights mounted on a rail under the radiator. They looked blue, like they were halogens, or something. Then they were gone, driving away up the street.

Somebody was screaming.

Mickey leapt into the road. Luckily, it was a side street and there wasn't continuous traffic. Any cars approaching would be going quite slowly, in the normal run of things. They would see the man lying prone on the asphalt, and the other man, a big guy with wide shoulders, bending over him, concerned. Other people were gathering; that would stop the traffic.

Jenner was still alive. He was breathing, but there was blood coming from his mouth.

Mickey did something he had been told never to do: move the patient. He got the victim under the arms and lifted him bodily out of the road. It was bad procedure, but this was no 'accident', and Mickey was suddenly convinced that Jenner wasn't safe out in the open. He got him under the canopy of the nearest shop, three doors up from the cafe called 'Miles'.

"I've called an ambulance," a helpful passer-by told him. The helper was bobbing up and down from one foot to the other.

Other people gathered round, but the self-appointed assistant shooed them back, to give the injured man some space.

Mickey dragged his own phone out. This was now something bigger than he could handle. He wanted his usual people around him. He put in a call to Regional Office, hoping to speak to the Duty Officer.

Out of the corner of his eye, he saw the vehicle. It was approaching again, right up on the pavement and bowling pedestrians and gawkers out of the way, its engine revving heavily as it ploughed along.

Mickey saw the row of spotlights. There was no doubt it was the same car, coming back to finish the job,

He took a step back and reached for his pocket, but there was no gun. Usually, he would have something. He would be armed. But he was off-duty. This was a favour for a friend, not part of his everyday duties.

That was it, then. The car was coming and he had nothing, nothing to defend himself with. Or Jenner.

Mickey was forced to stand back and watch the car career over the Doctor, crunching his body and moving on, completing the task the driver had set himself. There was nothing to see inside the vehicle, of course: the windows were blacked out, completely opaque.

People were screaming, but the sound hardly got through to Mickey. There were injuries, but then, there was an ambulance on the way, so that was a start, even if more would be needed. There wasn't much else he could do.

No, the real problem for Mickey was his own lack of judgement. He had got the situation completely wrong. He had misread the man. He'd concluded that Jenner was a fantasist, but that was incorrect.

Mickey looked up and saw his reflection in the shop window. His twisted face stared back at him.

Mickey, it was saying: how could you have been such an idiot?

CHAPTER TWO: New Faces

Less than a week later, Mickey was summoned to Regional Office to talk to his old boss, Captain Gibson.

"I've got a job for you," the older man said immediately. "It's a protection detail."

Mickey winced. Looking after somebody? Protecting them from harm? That's what Mr Jenner had wanted.

It was a grey, rainy day in Salford. Mickey had found the weather was matching his mood. He was down, drained, exhausted by life. He'd found it hard dragging himself out of bed that morning. The alarm clock had shrilled and he hadn't responded. Maybe he was a little depressed. The meeting with Dr Jenner was preying on his mind. He was going over and over it in his head, wondering if things could have been different, wondering if he could have saved the man somehow, if he had responded quicker.

Captain Gibson leaned forward. "Are you all right, Mickey?" he asked seriously. "How are you feeling?"

Mickey felt an air of unreality. His boss never talked about feelings. Why was he starting now?

Gibson pushed a folder across his desk. Mickey opened it and found himself looking at a picture of a middle-aged man with greying hair. He was smartly dressed in a suit and tie, with glasses. He wasn't smiling,

"He's Swiss," the Captain said. "He's flying in tonight. I've got some people meeting him at the airport and then they'll be taking him to a Safe House. It's too dangerous to try and put him in a hotel. There are too many people trying to get him."

"What's he done?" Mickey found himself asking.

"He's a scientist," a voice said behind him.

Mickey turned and saw Terry the technician standing there. He had slipped into the room somehow: Mickey hadn't even heard the door open, he was that distracted, lost in his thoughts.

"Good to see you, Terry," Mickey said, forcing a smile onto his reluctant face.

But he meant it. Terry had been away for almost a couple of years, taking a break from the intensive work that he was constantly being asked to do, solving problems, working all hours. It had been difficult to find a replacement, but when the Agency had, it was spooky that the next young man had the same nerdish appearance, wild hair, glasses. The only difference was the colour of his hair - it was blonde. Despite that, he found that people he worked with kept calling him 'Terry', in memory of the man he had replaced. The new 'Terry' then became Terry Two, when people remembered. In the face of such overwhelming odds, Terry Two dyed his hair red and became a technician who looked liked, talked like, and did the same jobs as his predecessor.

Then he got himself killed.

It happened, Mickey was thinking, in our line of work. The Captain, faced with the long, slow, tedious process of having to recruit yet another young brain box to do the technical tasks, gave in, and scoured the world for the original Terry. He offered bribes, more money, new equipment. Eventually the original Terry said that he would come back if they gave him a new lab, and the latest computers. The Agency was only too happy to agree. Okay, they said: 'state of the art' it is.

The old Terry said: "It's ironic, given what happened to your other friend, Dr Jenner."

Mickey shook his head. He didn't understand. What was Terry saying?

"This guy, Mr Marks," Terry said, pointing at the file, "he works for Crapanza too."

Mickey had no idea what Terry was saying. Jenner had said he was employed by a multi-national company, but he hadn't named it. Mickey picked up the file and flipped through the pages. This man, his new assignment, was a Senior Researcher for a pharmaceutical company, based in Geneva. That was the same as Jenner's? He didn't know.

"But they're on opposing sides of the fence," Terry said, baffling Mickey again. "I mean, Genetically Modified Food, GMOs. This man is an apologist. I've read Dr Jenner's blogs: he was a fierce critic."

Mickey frowned. But Jenner was being threatened. Because of his stance? So who is now threatening this Marks fellah, for taking the opposing line? Were there two sides of some kind of battle? Was it a war?

Captain Gibson was still being kind. "Why don't you two go for coffee?" he suggested. "You have things to discuss."

But Mickey had something more important to say to Terry, first, before conferring about the guy from Switzerland.

As soon as they got outside the boss's door, Mickey pushed a USB stick into Terry's hand.

"I got this from Jenner," he explained. "I'd like you to go through it."

Maybe Terry would understand it, he was thinking. If it was full of technical stuff, scientific reports, it would be useless for Mickey to try and understand it. He needed a scientific mind, and Terry was the best they'd got.

"It's off the clock," Mickey added. It had to be. Jenner had never been the business of WSB. It wasn't official.

Terry smiled grimly, as though he had some insight into what the memory pen might contain.

"Sure, Mickey," he said, nodding.

He'd be pleased too. This stick, this thing, might just contain the kind of things Jenner had been famously working on: research that might bring down the huge conglomerate once and for all, destroy the beast for ever.

Just what I had been hoping for, Terry was

thinking.

Meanwhile, at Manchester International Airport, the man called Marks had arrived.

Unfortunately, the agents from WSB were waiting at the main exit from Baggage Recovery and missed him. They didn't realise that he would be directed straight to the VIP Lounge, and come out of that door onto the main concourse.

Luckily for me, Marks was thinking, there was someone waiting for him, a short man with a sign: 'C.M. - Geneva'.

Mr Marks walked over, wheeling his small case on its own inbuilt wheels. The man offered to take the luggage, but his visitor refused. There was a laptop computer on top: he didn't want any chance of losing that.

"Follow me," the man said.

Marks wasn't worried. The man was smartly dressed in black and white and looked like a chauffeur. No doubt, he guessed, there would be a big car, perhaps a limousine, parked outside, waiting. It was what he was used to, travelling in style.

The man marched across the hall and straight into the Gents toilets. He held the door open for his guest.

"Change of plan," he told the boss. "You need to speak to Head Office. You've been recalled."

Firstly, Marks hesitated to enter a Rest Room with a complete stranger. Second, he couldn't believe that he would be told to abort his mission so soon, having only just landed in this Godforsaken country.

But, thirdly, the fact that he was being invited to contact Admin intrigued him. Who would have the nerve to issue such orders?

It was Yuri Lenkov, the new CEO, now ultimate boss of Crapanza. For now. Since last Thursday.

"Yuri," he said sweetly, to the scowling face on his mobile phone. "Always a pleasure."

The Russian looked long and hard at the screen in front of him, as if not sure who he was talking to. Then he barked.

"Marks, this little jaunt of yours must end," he ordered. "You have no authorisation from the Board."

"My visit was approved a long time ago, as part of Operation Alberta. When was it now - oh, perhaps in the summer, when you were away. You go away a lot, so I'm not surprised you missed it. It was before, when you were a junior Director only."

Mr Lenkov made a face. Well, those days are over, it seemed to be saying. I'm in charge now.

Marks was abrupt, almost rude. "Let's be clear," he went on, "your Russian money has bought you a place in this company, but you are not in charge of New Science. I am. I make the decisions about who I see and where I go."

"I want you on the next plane back. I don't

want any dissent. We are investigating your labs right now."

Marks sighed. "I didn't want to have to do this," he said, turned the phone around and tapped a little on the screen.

He didn't like to have to do this. They were in a toilet, for God's sake! Hardly a secure place to do business. Still, the short man had stationed himself at the door and was telling callers that there was a 'plumbing error' and they needed to use another facility. That meant that nobody - not even that flunky - could see what Mr Marks was doing or hear what he was saying.

He held his phone up. "Are you receiving the picture?" he asked pleasantly.

Mr Lenkov exploded in fury. Marks could see him come out from behind his desk, presumably to hustle anyone who was in the office with him out of the room. He cleared the place, so that no one could see what Marks had sent.

"Where did you get this photograph?" he demanded, taking his place again.

"Oh, I'm sure that's not important," Marks said smoothly. "The point is that I have incriminating evidence. No one will be surprised, of course. You are Russian. You like vodka and pretty women. Naked women. I have the pictures, which means you will now stop threatening me, in any way. You will leave me alone and continue your 'new broom' policy with someone else."

"How dare you - " the CEO spluttered. "What makes you think you can get away with this?"

Marks considered. When he spoke he knew he was being more than provocative: he was being racist. Insulting.

"Because you are Russian," he said. "Essentially, you are a coward. Oh, you might bluster and shout a little. But the fact is that your countrymen are right now dropping bombs on hospitals in Middle Eastern countries. That's not very brave, is it? It's quite easy to drops bombs from the sky, when you know that no one below has anti-aircraft weapons. It's also safe to bomb hospitals: you know there's no one there who can shoot back. It's murder, but there's no risk to you. That's what Russians do."

Mr Lenkov made a face, but he knew he was powerless to do anything concrete, from five hundred miles away.

Besides, he was being played. Mr Marks knew his weaknesses. Firstly, he had a taste for lewd women. Secondly, he felt like a second-class citizen because he was Russian. He knew that his money had bought him a position, but also knew that few people in Switzerland respected him, or his cash - knowing where it came from.

Mr Marks said: "So, summing up, I will not be taking orders from you. Not now, not ever."

His boss made one last try. "I am in charge of the most important pharmaceutical company -

" he began.

"Second to Sagar," the scientist interrupted. "Don't forget that Sagar International dwarfs us, by a factor of two to one."

It was the final insult. Mr Lenkov, angry and resentful, had no choice but to cut the line and live with his plans in tatters.

Now, Mr Marks was thinking, I need to move on from this nonsense.

Where are the damn British Security Service? And why aren't they looking after me?

Back at Regional Office, Terry was just getting back to his cubbyhole, cup of coffee in hand.

He had just spent a pleasant hour talking to colleagues in the canteen. There were some new faces there, and he was pleased to greet them. Others, old faces, were simply glad to see him back. There were warm words all around.

"I'm sorry about the circumstances," Terry said, pointing out that he was only there to replace a lost member of the team.

People shrugged, commiserated. What could you do? These things happen.

"At least it's saving us from Caulfield!" one quipped.

Terry queried that. He had been wondering why he hadn't seen the Deputy Director.

On an open-ended Compassionate Break, he was told.

The fact was that Caulfield had been badly

shaken by the way in which Terry Two died. Accordingly, he blamed himself. Quite right, most of the operatives thought: it was his fault. If he hadn't trusted the Chinese -

So the Deputy Director was on Gardening Leave and Captain Gibson was just having to struggle along without him.

Everybody grinned. I'm sure he will be managing just fine, one said sarcastically.

There was no love lost between anyone in the centre and the egregious Mr Caulfield. No, they weren't missing him at all.

Terry found himself smiling as he made his way back upstairs. No, he didn't like Caulfield either. He was sorry about the technician. It could so easily have been me, he realised. Still, that's the way the dust fell. Some, you lose.

He settled himself in to the small office and pushed the buttons to light up the bank of monitors in front of him. Terry had set his computer running, wearing itself out trying to decipher a cypher. There was no easy way to do it; it was just a matter of time and computing power. Terry was just going to have to wait.

That was his main computer. He had several laptops open on the desk. He selected one and pulled it over. It would do for examining the drive that Mickey had given him. He would just open the folders and flip through them, get an overview.

They were encrypted, all of them. Every folder, every file, was asking for a password.

Damn, Terry was thinking. This is going to take some time too.

He pulled a desk drawer open and tossed the memory stick in. There some others there. Terry pulled the one from Mickey back out and wrote some letters on the side, so that he wouldn't get it mixed up with the others. Which were - ?

They were all left behind by the previous Terry. This Terry knew that when he had time, he would go through them, identify the contents and label them. That was basic procedure. Of course, there never would be enough time, he knew that.

It was a strange desk, not at all modern. It was clearly not WSB standard issue, but maybe something that the other Terry had brought in from home. It looked a hundred years old. Maybe it had been acquired from a junk shop and Terry had polished it up. It didn't look like an expensive antique, exactly, but it was quirky, original. It said something about the owner.

Terry carefully laid Mickey's contribution in again, but as he withdrew his hand, it brushed up against the side of the drawer. A flap fell down. Terry stared. What the hell? There was a secret compartment, and inside - a memory stick.

That was unexpected. Terry carefully lifted the hidden USB pen from its hiding place and put it on the top of the desk. He turned it over. It seemed unremarkable. But it was labelled. A single word, and that made Terry's blood run cold.

It said: 'Crap'.

That could mean a number of things, Terry knew that. He didn't know Terry Two as a person, so had no idea what the man might have meant by the word. It could mean 'rubbish', and that USB pen would be where his junk was stored.

Then why hide it? If it was junk, then it couldn't be worth anything. Certainly, it wouldn't be worthy of concealment.

On the other hand, 'Crap' could be short for 'Crapanza', which would mean that the other Terry had an interest in the company too. Just like this Terry, the old one, come back to his previous life.

Now that was interesting, he was thinking. Maybe Terry Two has something on them.

I can't wait to find out.

Mickey hadn't reached the airport for one simple reason: he had been waylaid.

It was his own fault, he was thinking. He should have stopped long enough to ask Gibson and find out who his companion was going to be, the other operative that would be assigned to this case. There would be two of them, he knew that, plus the agents already at the airport, waiting at the Arrivals Hall. They always worked in two's, so two would be there now, and Mickey and his pal would meet them there, or at the Safe House, if they had already set off. That was Standard Procedure.

Mickey came down the stairs and out into

the yard at the back of the building, where the cars were kept. A white car had been pulled out from the line and was waiting by the gate with its engine running.

That's for me, Mickey was thinking, and walking towards it. He put a hand on the door handle, then froze.

The man inside leaned over and opened the door for him. He was smiling. Mickey wasn't.

"Hello, Dolf," he said quietly.

The man had changed. He had once had a full head of hair, but was now completely bald. His once handsome features seemed battered somehow, bruised and scarred. But he was still recognisable. It was still him. The traitor.

"Sit down," Dolf said quietly, "and I'll tell you a story."

Mickey sat in, it seemed impolite to refuse, but he wasn't keen to hear anything the former fellow agent was about to tell him.

It was an outlandish tale. Gibson had sacked Dolf and transferred him to the office in Leeds, but they didn't want him in Yorkshire either, not after what he had done. So they sent him out on field work, to follow a suspect from the Balkans. When the man went home, orders were to follow him. To Romania. Dolf had his passport and a company Credit Card, so he went.

There were planes and trains involved. Then the suspect got on a boat, and went out into the Adriatic to a small island off the coast. He checked in to a monastery, and started some kind of Retreat. Dolf was a few steps behind him, all the way.

"It worked," he said calmly.

What did? Christianity. I got it, Dolf said. I was converted. I got the message. I found the Lord.

Mickey thought that was extremely unlikely, but the next bit almost blew his mind.

"The buildings were crumbling and they were always short of money," Dolf said. "The only way they knew how to raise funds was to take part in illegal wrestling matches. I wanted to help. I begged them. So they let me join the team."

By this time, the car was on the road, heading out of Salford on the motorway and cruising around the Ring Road to Manchester International Airport. Mickey couldn't stop that happening. He had to work with this guy. For some reason the Captain had taken him back and assigned him to be Mickey's partner for this mission. He had been rehabilitated.

Maybe because of the religious thing.

Mickey doubted it. He couldn't quite see the reality in Dolf's picture of Roma camps and grown men throwing themselves at each other, covered in grease, under the moonlight, beside the camp fires. For money, illegal betting.

Maybe that explained the scars and the broken nose. Maybe it didn't. It seemed a trifle far-fetched.

"Look, Mickey, I've paid my dues," the other

man said. "I've seen the error of my ways, and I really need a second chance."

That was it, then. This was a test. Gibson had taken Dolf back, but only 'on trial'. The boss was giving him a fairly easy task, personal protection, to see how he went. Also to see whether he could work with the rest of the team, like Mickey.

"We've got a job to do," Mickey said. "Let's do that. I'm not promising anything."

"Nor me," Dolf said. "I've given my life to God, and he's making all the plans and giving the directions."

Mickey found that bit easy to believe, if by 'God' you meant a man called Gibson.

It was a simple journey around the motorway to the airport and the men were quiet for the rest of the time. The only noise was the sound of Mickey dialling through to the other operatives, the ones already there, meeting that Mr Marks fellah.

They weren't answering.

Mickey found that odd. Everybody was in touch with everybody these days. Mobile phones made communication easy and straightforward. But in this case, nothing was getting through. He put in calls, left messages, made texts.

He started to get worried. This shouldn't be happening.

They arrived, Dolf parked in an illegal bay, and they walked over to the Arrivals Hall. They stood under a large sign which said 'Meeting

Point' and looked around. There were plenty of people, but no one they recognised.

This wasn't right, Mickey was thinking. Just arrived, and things were going wrong already.

It was Dolf, he decided. He was a bad luck charm. This isn't going to end well.

Meanwhile, a few miles away, Melia was driving to meet with her friend the farmer, Mr MacLawn.

His place was at the end of a narrow and bumpy lane, with plenty of pot holes. The car's suspension was suffering.

Melia knew the place well, but hadn't been down that way for a number of years, not since the anti-fracking camp. That was a horror, nights under canvas, noise, dirt, no toilets. It had been scary and uncomfortable. From the point of view of the protesters, they got what they wanted, and drilling was stopped. But that was only temporary, Melia knew. The oil company would be back.

Meanwhile, Melia was going to see Tony, Mr MacLawn. He had been more than helpful, he had saved her bacon. Luckily for her he hadn't always worked the soil. During a long and distinguished career, he had served in the British Army. He knew Melia's story, admired her for it, and was willing to do anything to protect her and her commission.

Melia practically ran him over.

She was driving down a narrow piece of

track, high hedges on both sides, turned the corner and there he was, in the road.

She slammed on the brakes, pulling in to the side. The hedges had stopped. There were open fields on both sides of the metalled road, and Tony was standing in front of a sign on the left-hand side. That wasn't his property, she was thinking. His farm was on the right, as she remembered. That was correct: she could see his farmhouse further along, near some trees.

He didn't comment on her driving when she climbed out of the car. He looked really pleased to see her.

Melia noticed he seemed troubled.

"What's the notice?" she asked, trying to see what he was looking at.

"It's a 'Notice of Intent'," he told her, not bothering with formalities, since they already knew each other well. "Crapanza are announcing their intention to plant these fields over here with Genetically Modified wheat. They're calling it an experiment."

Melia nodded. That was bad? It was probably perfectly legal, wasn't it?

Oh yes, he agreed. They're very good at being 'legal'.

"In Canada," he told her, "they planted next to an innocent farmer's land and then took him to court. Pollen from their crops had blown on to his and contaminated his planting. They proved that, with DNA testing. They brought him before a Judge and accused him of 'stealing' their branded and patented variety. The court agreed with them: the testing 'proved' it, the Judge said. So he ordered that the Crappers could confiscate the whole of the farmer's crop and sell it for themselves. When they drove him into bankruptcy, they were there at the insolvency sale and they bought his land at a knock-down price. It was all very 'legal', Melia, and the company had high-priced lawyers to argue their case. All the farmer had was the truth, so he lost the argument."

"You think that's going to happen here?"

Farmer MacLawn gave a slow smile. His handsome face glowed with pride and determination. Melia liked that.

"Not if I can help it," he said grimly. "Come on. I want to show you something. Then we can talk."

They walked along the road towards his house, but before they got there they saw several barns. Tony led them into one.

"Look at this pile," he said, indicating half hundredweight bags stacked on shelves. Seeds, he said.

Melia noted various types of cereal - wheat, barley. Oats too, Tony said. She saw that they were all labelled 'S.I.'.

"Sagar International," the farmer explained. "I get all my seeds from them. They're a food and plant company based in Switzerland, a bit like Crapanza but nothing like as bad. I use all their products. It helps me avoid the other guys."

He pointed out shelves of herbicide in heavy, plastic bags. At the end, he said, in the plastic barrels, there were fungicides and insecticides. Chemicals, tons of them, all lined up and ready for next Spring's planting.

Melia was baffled. "You need all these chemicals?" she asked. She knew he had horses and pigs. Didn't he get slurry from them, muck that he could spread on his fields, good organic mix?

Tony laughed. "I use organic," he agreed, "but I've nowhere near enough to get the yields I need for the supermarkets."

It was a trap, he said. To sell my products, they have to be big, healthy and consistent. The only way I can guarantee that is to pump them full of chemicals when they start and souse them as they grow. Anything else, anything more 'natural', and they end up scabbed and twisted, at least some of them, and then there's nothing to sell and no guaranteed income.

Melia still didn't understand. Then he was already in the pockets of the chemical companies, she was thinking.

"I'm resisting," he said, "as much as I can. It's a constant battle. I want to stay independent."

It was a war he wasn't winning, she was thinking, but kept it to herself. She liked Tony, respected him. She wasn't rude.

"We'll walk down and get your car," he suggested, "then drive up to the house and I'll make you some coffee."

That sounded good. The day was bright but a little cold. Autumn had arrived and it was like an announcement that winter was on the way. She had been forced to wrap up warm that morning, putting on her winter jacket for the first time. It made her think of the need for her to look after herself now, now that she had someone else to worry about, apart from herself. The new life growing inside her. It still wasn't real, of course, not making itself felt. It was more like an idea, growing in her mind.

MacLawn walked briskly and she struggled to keep up. She kept getting distracted, looking around, at the countryside all about her. The leaves on the trees were turning and the colours were glorious. For a moment she envied the farmer his life out here, in the wild. Only a few miles from the city, perhaps, but it was like another world, still slightly wild and bracing.

"There's another car," she observed, looking down the lane.

Mr MacLawn bridled. They were parked in the road, not on his land, but he looked proprietorial. He hurried ahead.

Melia scurried to keep up. He seemed agitated and she didn't want him to do something silly.

The farmer stopped by Melia's car and looked over to the field behind the sign. There were two men bending down, scraping something on the soil. They stood up. One was holding a test-tube.

"Can I help you gentlemen?" Tony bellowed. They looked up, shook their heads and bent again. He started towards them.

This isn't your land, she wanted to remind him, but MacLawn was ahead of her, fuming and spoiling for an argument.

"And who would you two be?" he blustered, confronting them.

The men wore suits, smart suits, with expensive protective jackets on top and designer Wellington boots. They looked like business people. True, they had briefcases, but one had an aluminium specimen case too. It was open. Bottles showed.

The short one on the right said: "I don't think we have to introduce ourselves." He sounded formal, like a lawyer.

The other one, taller, more diplomatic, put a restraining hand on his arm. "I am happy to say Hello," he announced. "My name is Marks and I am employed by a company you may have heard of, given your trade. It's called Crapanza."

Mr MacLawn didn't hesitate. He strode forward, steely look on his attractive face, and launched a roundhouse punch straight into the jaw of Mr Marks, who shot backwards, flailing, losing his balance and falling onto the mud of the field.

This isn't what I wanted to see, Melia was thinking. I'm going to have to report this, one way or another.

CHAPTER THREE: New information

The next morning Mickey went to Dr Jenner's office.

He shouldn't have been there, but the truth was he had little else to do.

The team was in tatters. They had gone to the airport, missed meeting up with the expected arrival, Mr Marks, and were flailing around for hours. Mickey and Dolf simply added to the confusion. After a while they all went back to Regional Office and watched while Terry set up a 'Watch' protocol. Now, if Marks did anything - like make a phone call or spend some money on his credit card - it would trigger an alert. The team would then get to see where he was and zoom in to intercept him.

Meanwhile, all they could do was wait.

Strange, Dolf said sarcastically. He asked for our help to protect him and now he's hiding from us too.

Mickey shrugged. What could you do? You can reach me on my mobile, he said, and went home.

It didn't work. He couldn't settle, and he certainly didn't sleep. He couldn't relax. In the middle of the night he found himself looking at the business card that Dr Jenner had given him. It said 'JenCo', with an address in town. He decided to visit.

Mickey put on his smartest suit and got the tram into town. It made sense: parking was a nightmare and prohibitively expensive. He could get to the JenCo office, in Bridge Street in the middle of Manchester, and walk across the bridge to Regional Office later, if they needed him. If they didn't, he had no other plans for the day.

It was an old block of offices, maybe ten stories, but the insides had been completely gutted and replaced. Now it was all glass panels and muted lighting. Very twenty-first century, very High Tech, suitable for a top drawer consulting firm.

Mickey saw the name on the board in the lobby and took the lift to the sixth floor.

He found the employees in tears.

From the receptionist to the back office staff, they were all sitting around, all thought of work forgotten, crying.

Mickey tried to explain how he had met Jenner and he shared their grief.

"Not him," a lady in a while coat said quietly. "We've lost Mr Tom too."

Mickey stared in disbelief. Who? Who were they talking about?

Jenner had been killed and was not yet buried, for Goodness sake, but no, they had moved on, already. There were other partners in the firm, and one, Tom Leamington, had run his car off the road the night before, apparently.

"He has a cottage in Derbyshire," the woman

explained. "In the Peak District, up in the hills."

Mickey knew it. Go south out of Manchester and you came to the foothills of the Pennines before you got to Sheffield. He knew the roads, all twisty and turny, long drops on one side. He could imagine someone coming to grief. Easily.

Did anyone know what happened?

"Tight bend," the woman said. "Maybe a sheep in the road."

He was like that, she said. Caring. He loved animals and hated to see anything living hurt.

Mickey would have appreciated some more details, but they had none.

As for the company - he picked up a leaflet lying on the front desk. It said that JenCo offered 'consultancy, training and experimentation'. They did research, apparently, in the fields of agriculture, horticulture and aquaculture. They wrote reports, gave presentations and advised. A list of past clients followed: Crapanza was there, prominently. Also, something called 'S.I.'

The woman at the desk had tears pouring down her cheeks. "It's Tom's wife I feel most sorry for," she said.

"Yes, it must be terrible losing your husband," Mickey agreed.

"And your daughter."

They had a seven year old daughter, she said. A few months before, the poor girl had caught an unusual infection. It didn't respond to antibiotics and she had simply faded away. Tom had blamed himself, worried that he'd maybe passed on something he'd come into contact with. It was possible, the woman told Mickey. They experimented, ran laboratories.

Mickey helped himself to a cup of coffee from the machine in the corner of the Waiting Room. He offered to provide other people with drinks too, but they demurred, too consumed with grief. Mickey took a seat by the fish tank and watched it bubble.

What happens now? he wondered. Two senior partners in the firm lost in little more than a week. What do they do now? Where does JenCo go, without the 'Jen' and with so little of the 'Co' left?

And who would employ them?

At first, when talking to Dr Jenner about his work, Mickey had got the idea that the scientist worked for Crapanza directly. Now he saw that he was more than that. He was an outside consultant. An expert, at a distance.

If the good Doctor had fallen out with the firm, would they be interested in employing the survivors, the people who still worked at the old place? Mickey was thinking that those poor unfortunates would struggle to keep the business going, especially after losing two key figures.

Then something strange happened.

The main door opened and a courier came in, wearing reflective jacket and carrying his bicycle helmet. He placed a large envelope on the desk and demanded a signature for it. He seemed preoccupied, in a hurry, but the receptionist made him wait while she went inside and dragged a fat man in glasses out to deal with the visitor.

The man picked up the envelope, examining the stamps on the front. Then he signed the deliverer's chitty and passed it back, giving that man his satisfaction. The bike guy nodded and headed back for the door, towards the lift. He turned before he left.

He was in time to see the man in glasses lift the envelope in both hands and ceremoniously tear it in half, right down the middle. Then he flung the pieces back across the Reception desk and onto the expensive carpet.

Mickey stared, unable to understand anything that was going on, or why.

At about the same time, Melia was sitting on a hard chair in Manchester's biggest hospital.

She was on the second floor. It was where expectant mothers went.

Melia felt uncomfortable. Not just because of the unforgiving plastic of her seat, but because she wasn't sure if she was being silly, having arrived so early in the process. Maybe she should have left it a few weeks, she was thinking. After all, what could they tell her, at this stage? Still, Liv had suggested it. In fact, she had insisted.

Melia shook her head. What did Liv know about motherhood? Her young cousin was as inexperienced as she was.

There was one boon to it: you got as many days off as you wanted. Melia had simply phoned in, mentioned that she was 'off sick', then, when the sweet girl in Personnel asked personal questions, she simply went into the details of morning sickness.

That was sufficient. It's enough to scare anyone, Melia reflected, man or woman.

A man came and sat down on the same row of seats, four along from Melia.

That was odd. It was a man. Melia looked around, and noted the scarcity of the fair sex. It was all women, waiting, sat, unmoving, philosophical. Who was this stranger? There for his wife, perhaps? His girlfriend?

"Melia?" the young man asked, turning her way.

She looked at his boyish demeanour, his curly hair and thin face. He looked vaguely familiar. He knew her?

He moved one seat closer to her. There were still a few to go, but it was clearly a gesture of familiarity.

"I'm not sure we have ever been introduced," she suggested, and he nodded at that. He agreed.

Then he pulled out a photo from his inner pocket and gently unfolded it. It showed a family. One face was familiar to Melia.

It was Snoopy.

Perhaps it was her condition, her racing hormones and insecurities, but the picture brought tears to Melia's eyes.

'Snoopy' was the name she gave to Greg Snopes, a young agent who had worked with her for several years, earlier in the decade. He was a new trainee and Melia had taken him under her wing for a time. They had developed a rapport, and she became like a big sister to the youngster. She was devastated when he was killed in action, blown up by a car bomb.

"I'm a Snopes too," the man on the seat said. "Greg was my cousin. We were a close family. We grew up together."

Melia felt emotions washing over her, anger, regret, and, most and worst of all - guilt. It was her car. The bomb had been meant for her, but she made the mistake of lending him the keys and letting him drive it. Strangely, given recent developments, the perpetrators were Russians, unofficial ones, but ex-Security and ruthless nevertheless, completely uncaring.

She blamed herself. It had given her many sleepless nights over the years. She didn't feel much better now.

The man said: "I know that Greg looked up to you. He talked about you many times. He was, I suppose, in love with you, a little. I know that none of my family blame you for what happened. It was all very unfortunate."

Melia dabbed at her cheeks with a paper hanky, then used her sleeve when that got saturated. This man, this Snopes, pulled a white linen handkerchief from his jacket pocket and handed it over, smiling ironically. He wanted to be of assistance.

But what was he doing there? How did he

know she would be there? What was going on?

"Please forgive me," he said. "This is all completely unprofessional. I work in the lab downstairs, processing samples. I'm up and down to Gynae all the time, and I saw your name on the Appointments list. I felt I just had to come over and say something."

Melia tried to control her sniffles. "I'd like to talk to you some time, about Greg," she said.

"I'd like that," he said. "Look, why don't I give you my card? My mobile number is there. You think about it, check your Diary and give me a call when you have some free time. It has to be out of here, far away from a medical setting. Look, don't worry about your confidentiality: I haven't looked at your Records, and we won't discuss such matters anyway. We can meet up in the city centre, maybe, share a coffee and talk about old times. It would be good."

I live in the city centre, Melia was thinking, then checked herself. No, it wouldn't be appropriate to invite him back to her flat, not at this stage. Who knows, maybe they could be friends one day, but right now, it would be so easy to get the signals wrong.

He stood up, pressed a card into her hand, held it for a moment, as if reassuring, then left, walking back up the corridor and out of sight. He gave her a small smile, a little look of solidarity. He wasn't trying it on, she could see that.

The next men were different.

One sat down on each side of her. They

wore suits and close fitting overcoats. They had hats in their hands.

"We'll just walk out of here, nice and easy," the one on her right said.

Melia was scandalised. You know how long it took me to get this appointment? she was thinking. And I haven't been seen, yet. I want a doctor's opinion, and I sure as hell aren't 'walking out' until I get an examination, at least.

"You don't want me to get awkward," the thick man said again, grating the words out under his breath.

"State your business," another voice said.

Melia looked up. It was Terry, from Regional Office. How did he know she was there? How many people did? Was it everyone's business now, her obstetrics problems and tests? She was fuming. This was too much!

The ugly man on Melia's left stood up. He was very tall and very square.

"You're a technician," he told Terry. How did he know that? "Leave while you can," he advised.

Terry was carrying a rucksack on his back, the sort that would hold a laptop computer and accessories. He dumped it on the floor in front of his feet and pulled back one of the zips on a pocket. He pulled out a small black rectangular box.

The standing man looked and sneered: "You gonna buzz me with your Remote?" he asked jocularly.

"It's a Tazer," Terry said, and rammed it directly into the man's groin.

There was a buzzing noise and the smell of burning flesh. The man stifled a pained groan and fell over, onto the washable floor.

The other man stood, walked around Terry, retrieved his partner and helped him to his feet. They retreated.

"I've been trying to contact you," Terry said to Melia reproachfully and sat down beside her in the empty seat.

Melia was angry. "What do you want with me, Terry?" she demanded. "What are you doing here?"

Coincidentally, in the same building, but on a higher floor, the man called Marks was lying in a hospital bed.

He thought his visit was more or less unnecessary too, but his companion had insisted. Mr Marks had been punched and knocked over. That wasn't so bad, lying in the rich earth of an English farm, but when he tried to get up, he found he couldn't. His balance was all over the place and he kept falling over again. After several attempts failed, an ambulance was called.

Luckily for Farmer MacLawn the health emergency took all attention away from the fact he had caused the problem. Perhaps the police should have been called at the same time, but no one thought to do it. Melia was there too, but she didn't suggest it. When the ambulance left, and the second man in the suit climbed into his big car and drove off, following it, she turned to her friend the farmer, they hugged, and he went off about his business. She left.

That was the day before. Mr Marks spent a restless night. He slept fitfully but still couldn't get out of bed and had to be helped by nurses when he wanted to pee. It was demeaning. Still, being an E.U. citizen, he wasn't expected to pay for such care.

He refused breakfast but managed to drink several cups of coffee. He started to feel better.

A man in a white coat with a stethoscope around his neck came into the room and examined the patient's chart. Another one in the endless roll of doctors calling. Luckily, he was thinking, I am the only sick person in the room. I get all the attention.

The medical person turned and busied himself at the sink. When he turned around again, he had a glass in his hand.

"I want you to drink this," he said calmly. "I think it will help."

"What's in it?"

The man in the white coat seemed confused. He obviously wasn't used to people asking questions.

Mr Marks stated: "I work in the pharmaceutical industry. I know every chemical in common use today, and I'm working on several that may become part of your repertoire in the future. It's a perfectly reasonable question."

"Just drink the fluid," the man said, irritably. Unjustifiably, his patient was thinking.

"Don't drink it," a voice said.

Two men came bustling into the room. One of them was called Dolf, but Mr Marks wouldn't have known that.

The other backed the man in the white coat up against the sink, roughly, disrespectfully.

It was almost as though the newcomers didn't believe that he was a real doctor.

"British Security Services," Dolf announced. "We've had a hell of a job finding you, Herr Marks."

It was almost as though the industrialist had been avoiding them, and nobody could think why that would be.

Still, he had been forced to provide details for the admin staff when they checked him in. It hadn't been entered on Medical Records straight away, but when the clerks did so, this morning, a bell went off in Terry's cubicle. After all, it was standard practice: you're looking for someone who's missing? Of course they might turn up in A and E !

Mr Marks scoffed. "If people are pretending to be who they are not," he said, "how do I know who you are?"

"The code word is 'Hospital'," Dolf said. It had been chosen before it had any significance.

Marks nodded. Yes, well, that was right, anyway. Perhaps he could put himself in these people's hands.

He said: "You know I have important work to do? People to see, contracts to sign. Why should I go with you?"

Dolf was holding the glass in his hand. He held it up to the light, but there was no way of telling what it contained.

"As long as unknown people are trying to poison you - " he suggested.

Marks shrugged. "Not 'unknown' at all," he snapped.

He knew precisely who was behind it. Trying to poison him? Who would try to poison him? It was a woman's weapon. Who would stoop so low to such a dastardly scheme? Only a Russian! It's what they did. When the Kremlin wanted to kill one of their ex-spies living in London a few years ago, they sent over a container of radioactive poison. No one had been caught for the crime, arraigned or charged. That was cowardice too, but poison? It was the work of a fearful and weak individual.

"Sure, I'm coming with you," the Swiss scientist announced. "Get me some clothes, if you please."

Dolf went off to find a nurse and get that organised.

He wasn't happy. Why am I doing this? Where's Mickey? We were meant to be part of a team. Why couldn't he be found? I had to get one of the other operatives to help me out. It wasn't fair.

Dolf wanted to work with Mickey. Again.

Like the old days.

At the same time, at her house in Swinton, Cousin Liv was doing research.

It was what she was good at. For the last few years she had been studying and tutoring at Salford University. She had covered a number of subjects in that time, but Social Policy was one of the ones she specialised in. When Melia told her about Crapanza, she was intrigued. It was Half Term, the students were away, she had time to look into it.

For the farmer too, of course. It was because of his fears about chemicals that Melia had been dragged in, and Melia had dragged Liv in. That was the way it happened. Liv didn't approve. What was this 'friendship' between her cousin and the farmer? It didn't matter that MacLawn was, in fact, a former agent - which gave the two adults something in common. No, what bothered Liv was that Melia had something more important to worry about now, the baby. Why swan around with random men?

She needed to settle down, work out who she was going to live her life with, and build a nest for the three of them.

Fire retardants.

Well, that was fascinating. Looking at the history of the company, what was now called Crapanza started out as a small chemical company called 'Stanza' in Buffalo, New York. That made sense; it was on the shipping route from the Great Lakes to the sea, and an ideal place to drop off supplies. But then, once they expanded, they moved to Southern California. Fair enough, still with access to ocean-going ships and within easy reach of raw materials from Latin America. So why leave? Why set up the office in Switzerland? Because of the law suits, apparently. Crapanza wanted to be in an independent jurisdiction, outside US law.

The problem was fire retardants. California was big on them, passing a series of laws in the 1970s. The chemical company had a boom time, providing the liquids to impregnate cloth. It was a good thing, everyone said, it helped to save children's lives. Then years passed and not one firefighter came forward to say, 'Thank God for the fire retardant, it saved this family'. Or that. Or the other. Not one. Meanwhile, researchers in Universities found a link between the chemicals used and breathing difficulties in children. So, there was a face off: which was more important - saving the children's lungs or stopping them from getting burnt?

The problem for the company was that people concerned with asthma and bronchitis wanted to ban the fire retardants totally, and it was big business, big profits. Stanza hired a PR firm and funded a huge media campaign, mostly exploiting the good looks of charming young cherubs begging, 'Please don't let me die in a fire'. It was heartbreaking.

They won. The courts threw out the efforts

to try and get retardants banned. Stanza was saved. Then parents with children who couldn't breathe properly all got together and launched a combined suit to get damages. The company upped sticks.

Legally, they became Swiss. Walking around the USA you wouldn't have noticed much difference; the refineries and laboratories were still there, across the US, but different logo, different name. The profits now flowed east, to Geneva.

Liv was shocked. It was so blatant, so underhand. She couldn't understand how business people could do stuff that was perfectly legal, and yet so obviously wrong. And yes, it was important. It was about life and death. Not just in terms of fires and preventing them. The fire retardants had also been linked with infertility and birth defects.

Good Grief, that could be Melia! Liv was thinking. She felt something personal, that her cousin's baby might be affected by such careless use of chemicals. Of course, that wouldn't happen, she found out, reading on. The chemicals listed had later all been banned in Europe and India. The attempt in the US to get them banned hadn't worked, so Americans still had the same chances of being ill. In fact, as it said later, no dangerous substances ever got banned there, even asbestos!

Liv took notes on her small pocket computer. I'll print this out later, she was thinking.

Then the doorbell rang.

It might be double-glazing salesmen, she was thinking. It might be Mormons. It could be somebody trying to get me to change my energy supplier. Whoever it was, it was disturbing her work. However, something made her go and open the door anyway.

It was a 'Five-a-Day' woman.

"Are you getting all the fruit and vegetables you need?" she asked brightly.

Her badge said she was a member of Salford's Health Improvement Task Force. She had a message for the unhealthy.

There wasn't anyone like that here. Liv was a regular at the gym. She ran, she swam, she ate fresh food.

The woman was preaching to the converted.

Since Liv was in research mode, she decided to become the one asking the questions.

"Why five?" she asked the lady, turning her leaflet over in her hand.

The woman actually smiled. "You know, a lot of people ask me that question, and mostly I lie. I see I can tell you the truth. The fact is, the government had to find a number, something memorable. So they picked five. It could have been four, or seven. But look, five seems achievable, right? All you have to remember is to pick five portions of fruit or veg, every single day."

"And you improve your health?"

"Round here? Yes!" she chuckled. I've met people, she confided, lots of people, who say they never eat vegetables. Never. Some wouldn't look at a piece of fruit, either. It was worrying, but what could you do? They're adults. They have to decide.

"But you do?" Liv asked. You take your own advice, right?

The woman suddenly looked grim. She was shaking her head, disagreeing with her own propaganda.

"I'll tell you the truth," she said. "What's the point of nibbling fruit that should be good for you, but is covered in chemicals? Most of the stuff you buy from the supermarket is, soaked in the stuff. You can rub your apples under the tap, but it won't scrub off that layer. You might as well put poison in your mouth, that's what you're doing, after all."

Liv decided to take a stab in the dark.

"What do you think of a company called Crapanza?" she asked sweetly.

"I despise the bastards!" the woman retorted.

Later that afternoon, Mickey went to Jenner's funeral.

He couldn't understand why it had taken so long to get organised. Sure, it was a violent death and there would have had to be a Post Mortem, but the cause of death was clear: multiple injuries from contact with a vehicle. That much was irrefutable. As to who did it, and exactly why, the police were saying they had no leads. Not yet. Maybe they would find some evidence. Maybe. Mickey wasn't hopeful.

The sad event was scheduled in Agecroft Cemetery, one of the biggest and most important in Salford. It was down by the River Irwell, along the road from the Football Academy. It wasn't a part of the city that Mickey was used to going to, but it was fairly close to his flat in North Salford, so he knew the area and found the place without trouble.

It was a cold day. It was autumn, and people were wrapped up warm. Faces were hard to recognise, behind scarves.

Still, Mickey was impressed to see that there was a large turn-out. This man had been popular, then. He had colleagues, of course, but other people from the business community were there, and civic leaders.

And criminals.

Mickey went over to the small clump of men in black suits, waiting under the trees by the corner for the cortège to arrive.

"What are you doing here, Scarrett?" he demanded.

Their paths had crossed before. The gangster had nearly got Melia killed. He was a mean and vicious killer.

"Maybe you had something to do with the Doctor's death?" Mickey suggested, his voice ugly.

"I'd kill my own cousin?" the bullet headed

criminal said calmly. He drew Mickey aside.

"You've got contacts in the police," he told him. "Anyone talking? We know who did this?"

Mickey took a deep breath. He was always amazed how small the Salford community was. Everyone seemed to know everyone, and most of them were related to each other. He shouldn't have been surprised, really, that Jenner had relatives.

"I don't care what you think of me," the drug dealer said. "On this we can agree. We get the men who did this. Yes?"

Mickey nodded, meekly. Sure, he wanted to find the killers. For Mickey, it was personal, a grudge.

"And the others," the gangster said, and looked away, gritting his teeth.

Mickey stopped, surprised. What had he said? He was talking about Jenner's colleague, in the office? He was dead.

"No, our Dr Jenner had a nephew. He died in a swimming 'accident' on the canal. But it wasn't an accident."

Mickey drew a breath. What was he saying? Scarrett was laughing at Mickey's naivete.

He said: "If you want to give a guy a warning, you kill one of his family first. A nephew is a good place to start."

Mickey was shocked. This was the way modern business was conducted? How did he know this information?

"It's the sort of thing I would do," he told

Mickey.

It was a cold day. Scarrett drew his expensive coat around him and went back to wait with his gang. But before he left he reached into an inside pocket and brought out a card. It had various phone numbers on it. Call me, he told Mickey before he went.

Mickey looked around to see if there was anyone else that he knew. He was anxious to find a friendly face.

He saw a lady getting out of a car, over on the side of the road leading to the main gates of the crematorium.

It was Melia.

Mickey hurried over. He hadn't seen the girl for weeks. Where had she been hiding? He'd called, left messages.

The man holding the car door was familiar too. It was Terry. Mickey was halted in his tracks. What were they doing together?

"Good to see you," he said, recovering himself. He meant Melia.

"Hey, take it easy, big guy," Terry admonished. His tone was patronising. Mickey was stunned again.

What was Terry doing, telling him how to treat the only woman in his life? His on/off girlfriend of many years.

"She's going to need to take it slow," Terry said, as if that explained anything. He held out an arm for Melia.

What's going on? Mickey was wondering,

confused. She was hurt? She had met some problems on the job?

"She's pregnant," Terry blurted. "You're going to have to get used to it, Mickey."

Mickey stared, lost for words.

Nobody had told him anything, he was thinking, baffled and hurt at the same time.

What else did he need to know, now that this bombshell was out in the open?

CHAPTER FOUR: More surprises (none good)

A few days later, Mickey found his way to a water treatment plant in Lancashire.

It hadn't been a good few days.

Mickey was on edge, nervous, anxious about what was happening - and not happening. The job he was meant to be doing - baby-sitting a visiting dignitary - was boring and repetitive, without any of the supposed threats materialising.

The other job he had taken on - the frustrating investigation into why Dr Jenner had been assassinated - was a bit more lively, but still producing no results. He felt he was going round in circles, getting nowhere, in circles he didn't really understand. It was a different world to his usual life.

That was why he chose to drive to the water treatment plant. It was the last place Jenner had been working, before he died.

Mickey had an address and a postcode, but it was baffling: it wasn't on any maps. It couldn't have been more than a hundred metres from the East Lancs Road, a busy thoroughfare, but it was behind hedges and trees, completely hidden. Mickey didn't enjoy driving down the narrow lanes to find it. He didn't know what was around the next corner. It might be unpleasant.

Like the day before. He had been coming

home, back to his house in North Salford. It was late in the afternoon, but already getting dark. The clocks had gone back and it was darker earlier, he noticed. It didn't improve his mood.

He pulled his car into his drive and got out. Then a motorbike came tearing up the street and there were two loud bangs.

Mickey found himself flattened against his car, down on one knee. It was an automatic reaction. He looked around, and saw two young kids on the pavement opposite. They were throwing bangers and lighting fireworks. Kids. It was a week after Bonfire Night but they still had their stash of fireworks to use up. That's all it was, then. Them. The motorbike passing was a coincidence but it made Mickey jump and reminded him of the unpleasant sight of seeing Dr Jenner gunned down. He didn't need reminding.

Still looking for the treatment plant, Mickey consulted his sat nav. It told him to turn down a street into a housing estate. He proceeded through that and was faced by a track, an untarmaced surface, full of potholes. He drove gingerly down that, rounded a bend and came face to face with a gate.

There was a sign and a man standing inside a little wooden hut. Yes, this was definitely the place.

Mickey stopped his car and went over to the man. He told him his business and said he had an appointment. The man went into his shack and picked up a phone. A few minutes later he opened the gate and Mickey pulled through.

There was a general car park on the right. Mickey pulled his car into that and saw a man in a high vis jacket walking towards him. The man saw him and waved him into a slot to park. Mickey got out and shook his hand.

The man was young and had that preoccupied air of an engineer or an architect. He said nothing about himself, but led Mickey into a block of temporary portakabin offices. At the end of a row of doors, he opened the last one.

It said 'JenCo' on the door.

"This is where they used to work," the man said gruffly.

Mickey paused. 'They'? If they were 'they', then who are you? he asked the kid.

The young man brushed back his floppy hair and screwed his eyes up behind his glasses.

"I work for Termack," he said awkwardly. "We share the building. I'm working on waste processing. They were on the clean water research, as far as I know. We didn't talk much. They did testing, mostly. I'm on installation."

Mickey shook his head. He wasn't sure what he was hearing. 'JenCo' was the company he was aiming to research. Surely they could all agree on that.

How many? Mickey asked. How many of them were working on this project?

"Three," the young man said, fairly convincingly. "Two partners and the apprentice.

The youngster left after Geoff had his accident. That left Dr Jenner, on his own for a while. I was sure he was going to bring some other people in, then."

Mickey nodded his head. Okay, that made sense. The 'other partner', the one who had an accident? Yes, he had been told about that when he visited their office in Manchester. That was right -

No, it wasn't. The man they talked about there was called Tom. This one was called Geoff.

Mickey's skin began to crawl. Something was bothering him.

"This accident," he began slowly, "exactly what kind of 'accident' was it? What happened?"

The young man squirmed. He didn't seem to want to talk about it. It was like dragging the information out of him.

"He got locked in the steam room," he reported. "The door was faulty, we all knew that. We didn't know the valves were loose, of course, and that's what really finished him. The process is timed to go off every hour and Geoff was caught inside."

"Why do you need steam?"

"To clean the pipes," he said, as if everyone knew that. "The steam comes out at four times atmospheric pressure. It can be really tricky. The person in charge is on contract from the suppliers. They are the only people who know how to regulate it properly."

Where was he? Mickey demanded.

"He has to have a day off, every now and again."

Mickey sat down on a chair. He suddenly felt very old, deflated. What was happening? Everyone connected to Jenner, whether colleague, friend or family, was dropping like flies. The doctor was like the Angel of Death, the Grim Reaper. Dangerous to know.

"You want to have a look around?" the kid asked. "I'm making tea. I'll get you a cup and then we can do the tour."

Mickey was glad to be left alone. He scanned the desk, opened drawers, looked in filing cabinets. He examined the print-outs stapled to the notice boards and looked at the tomes stacked along the bookshelves.

In truth, he had no idea what he was looking for. It all seemed so orderly, well organised. So ordinary. Where were the clues? What had Jenner been doing that was so bad it had got him killed? Who objected to his work, and why?

After a cup of tea, the young man handed Mickey a high visibility jacket and a hard hat. He gave him gloves and protective goggles. God, Mickey was thinking - we're going into the jaws of death?

Nearly. They followed the water, from its input near the gate, to the first tower where it was sieved and solids separated; to the second tower where it went through sand; then carbon filters; then ultraviolet light. As they came around the corner of the third tower, Mickey was shown a squat building with smoke rising from an aluminium tower. The steam room.

"It's a bomb, that boiler," the kid said cheerfully. "If it ever blows, it will take us all out."

Nice. Mickey nodded, not sure what any of it meant.

"Let's go up and see the pumps," his guide suggested. "They're German, precision made. A superb investment."

He stepped aside to let Mickey clamber up the metal stairs attached to the outside of the large building. When we get to the top, the youngster told him, we can look down and see the rotors. That pressurises the whole system, the kid said.

The water gets treated, Mickey knew that. Jenner had told him. But the scientist had also said that the process didn't get to grips with the medications in the mix, the antibiotics and hormones. He would ask about that, he decided. Before he left.

As he came out onto the platform, thirty metres up, Mickey leaned forward to take the grab handle in front of him and it came away in his hand. He staggered to one side and flipped over the guard rail. Desperately, he reached out and clamped a hand on the top railing. His body was dangling, but he wasn't falling. If the kid would just stop screaming like a girl and give him an assist, he could pull himself back up, he reasoned. It was unfortunate, but he hadn't gone over the side, like some might.

Still, it was strange. Either steel screws had come loose on their own, or they had been loosened.

Was this designed to be another one of the 'accidents' dogging Dr Jenner and his crew?

Meanwhile, Mr Marks was taking care of business in the Unit's Safe House.

He was glad he had finally agreed to go with them and accept their hospitality. It wasn't luxurious - like one of his usual four or five star hotels that he favoured - but it was comfortable, and, since he was the only guest, he was well looked after.

Besides, he had been able to get out in the last few days and take some meetings. Afterwards, they drove him around for a while, in case anyone was following, then brought him back here. He was grateful for that. He didn't want people to know where he was staying: he'd had trouble with gatecrashers before, and it had all ended rather unhappily.

Luckily, the broadband connection was fast. Herr Marks had several people he needed to speak to via his laptop computer, and the video was faultless. Right now, he was checking his emails and following the links to documents and reports.

What the hell? He looked at the picture staring back at him. It was a WSB agent, name of Amelia Hartliss.

Now this, he was thinking, this is embarrassing. After all, these people were his hosts.

The report said that they had spotted Melia visiting a farm in one of their target areas. The undercover people had made investigations and established that she was an old friend of the farmer. He was a known trouble-maker, so the staff had tried to make contact with Ms Hartliss. They had met with her at a hospital in Manchester, but been chased away by one of Melia's colleagues. It had been a painful encounter, apparently. That made Marks chuckle.

Still, the rest didn't. He fired off an angry Memo and made clear, abundantly clear, that the field team were to leave this woman alone from now on. He had met her, of course, (but that encounter was embarrassing and he didn't want to mention it). Instead, he simply said that he was in place within WSB already. It was the foremost anti-terrorism unit in the whole of British Security, of course, and it was a conflict of interest to have people from his company harassing one of their employees. It wouldn't do him any good at all.

It was almost as bad as this Jenner nonsense.

Someone had killed Dr Jenner, a man that Crapanza had been arguing with, so naturally the company would be getting the blame.

But they hadn't done it.

He didn't know how many times he had told his Board that yes, Jenner, was a problem, and yes, he would take care of it. But when something happened - it wasn't him. Mr Marks was working on something a little less dramatic, like suing the guy or blackmailing him. Or even bribing him. Anything to shut him up. Driving over him with a car, well, that wasn't Mr Marks's style.

Someday, maybe soon, he was going to need to find out who was behind the murder. He was intrigued.

The door opened and a man came in with a tray of tea things. It wasn't the usual servant. It was Dolf.

Mr Marks made a point of closing his computer, so the screen couldn't be seen, then he waited while Dolf poured the tea.

"I thought we could have a little chat," he said to his responsibility from Switzerland.

"I wondered how long it was going to take," the executive commented.

He accepted the cup of tea and smiled when Dolf pushed a plate of chocolate biscuits his way. Very good. Belgian, he was thinking. Still, he knew what went into those products - his company made the sweeteners. He demurred the offer.

"I haven't said anything," Dolf told the man. "Your assistant is very pushy, I noticed that, but I let him talk. I haven't volunteered anything. I wanted the opportunity to sit down with you first. What do you know?"

"I know," Mr Marks said, sipping his tea and

enjoying it, "that 'Hospital' may or may not be a WSB codeword, but for that week I arrived, it was a Crapanza codeword. I concluded from that interaction that you are one of us."

Dolf giggled. "Not at all," he said, laughing. "I'm an outside consultant, not on your payroll. You give me money, I give you service."

Ah, the British, Marks was thinking. So subtle. No wonder they can be such a problem.

"What do you want me to do?" Dolf asked casually.

"Today? Nothing," was the reply. "But beware, we live in interesting times. As you know, the U.S. election is this week. Whatever the result, the fallout for a multi-national like ours will be intense. We have people over there working on it, covering all the angles, all the doors and windows. But I'm here. Britain is a big problem for us at the moment, with all that anti-fracking nonsense and the ban on G.M. foods. We have to find ways to get around the restrictions and open new paths to Free Trade, for the benefit of all trading partners in the West. Don't worry, we will need your insider knowledge, but not immediately."

Dolf nodded. He could wait. He sipped his tea. This was one my easier assignments, he was thinking.

Oh, and he did regret having to lie to Mickey, but what the hell: a man has to make a living.

Melia, too, was taking tea.

In her case, she was in a cafe in Irlam, which was surprisingly near to her friend's farm. It wasn't an obvious choice, but when she was pressed to come up with a rendezvous in a hurry, it was the first choice that sprang into her mind.

She was meeting the man called Snopes. The cafe was an ideal place: it was public, very open and old-fashioned. The tea was served in flowery cups and there were tablecloths on the table. It was quite retro, vintage, and Melia was hoping that would discourage this Snopes from getting the wrong idea. She wanted to talk to him, that was all, about his dead cousin.

It was also a very popular spot, and Melia had been forced to book a table. They sat them near the window.

The time was past lunch, but Melia hadn't eaten, so she ordered soup and a sandwich. Snopes had cake.

They drank tea and tried to make small talk. This wasn't much use, Melia was thinking, and steered the conversation.

"Greg was my trainee," she told the man. "I was his mentor for a long time, over a year."

He nodded. "He admired you, looked up to you. He said you taught him a lot."

I tried to teach him how to look after himself, but I didn't do a very good job, she was thinking. It didn't protect him.

"He knew the risks," Snopes assured her. "He never talked about it - he wouldn't - but his commitment was clear."

Yes, he did his job, she replied. And he did. He was quite patriotic. He loved the idea of defending his country.

"So, tell me again: who killed him?"

Melia was taken aback by this directness. What could she say? They were Russians, but not the current regime. They were old-fashioned, like this cafe, unreconstructed KGB. Living in the past, they were still fighting the Cold War.

She allowed herself to get distracted by the arrival of the food. She fussed over sipping the soup, adding salt and pepper.

What could she tell him? It was natural he would want to know the details, but she didn't want to reveal too many pieces: if he put the jigsaw together, it might reveal what she didn't want to have to admit - it was all her fault.

The door banged open, cutting into her thoughts. Melia stared. It was Liv standing there.

Liv saw them and came over. She pulled out one of the spare chairs and sat down. Melia was shocked.

"Oh, do please join us," she said sarcastically.

Liv seemed too bothered to notice. "Cousin," she said. "Live in Salford. Tracked you down."

"I'm a cousin too," Snopes said easily, smiling, comfortable. Any friend of Melia's was a new friend to him.

The waitress came over, as they did in olden days, and insisted on taking an order. Liv asked for coffee. In a tea-shop.

"To what do we owe this intrusion?" Melia said, snapping again. She was trying to assert her displeasure.

"Little Mattie is autistic. It's official," she announced. "They've done the tests and printed the results. We've got an answer."

Melia searched her memory, but a 'Mattie' didn't pop into view. A cousin? A younger relative?

Liv said, explaining to the man at the table: "I call him my 'cousin', but it's through marriage, so he's no relation at all, really. Which is fortunate, in a way. They tried to say it was genetic, at first, so that seemed like good news for me and Mel. We don't share any DNA with the kid. He's on a completely separate family tree. They're from Bolton, too. Miles away."

Snopes looked interested. Why? Melia thought. Why would he care? Unless this was some special interest of his? He was in healthcare, anyway, as he had said. Did he know something about autism, its roots, its causes and its progression?

Or was he interested in Liv. She was a good-looking woman, even if a little eccentrically dressed today, with mixed colours and wild hair over her collar. She had good bones, Melia had always thought. Very pretty, when nicely done up.

Liv ploughed on. "It's chemicals, isn't it? I knew they might be trouble, living in Runcorn, like they did."

Near the chemical plants? Melia was thinking. Liv had never mentioned that before. Was it relevant?

Snopes shook his head. He seemed to disagree, showing his specialist knowledge after all.

"There have been studies in the U.S.A.," he informed them both, "that might suggest a link. But not here in U.K."

Liv said: "Yeah, I know that. Still, I work at Salford University and I've been talking to people. They're telling me that it could be true."

Snopes looked about to say something else, but he clamped his lips closed. He would save it till later, he decided.

"It's the environment," Liv declared, convinced by her research. "And it's the big chemical companies that are to blame. People like you've met, Melia. That man you were telling me about. What was his name? Marks, was it? From Crapanza?"

Melia frowned. No, she didn't think she had mentioned someone by that name. Where had Liv got that idea from?

Liv noted her confusion. She also noted the man's reaction. When she said 'Marks', he practically jumped out of his chair!

Now why would that be? she wondered.

Meanwhile, down on the farm, MacLawn was welcoming two new visitors.

"Get out of here!" he shouted. "Get back in your car and don't come back."

The men, smartly dressed in suits and ties, were unfazed. They had encountered negative reactions before.

"We really want to hear what we've got to say, sir," they suggested, wheedling.

Mr MacLawn took a deep breath. Yes, he was a little intrigued. Why would Crapanza bother to send these lawyers?

"I know what you're going to say," he insisted. "Your company is planting up a field next to mine. You're going to call it 'experimental', but when blossoms blow over and contaminate my crops, you're going to take me to court."

They nodded. Yes, that was Phase One, they silently agreed. He knew that much anyway.

But if asked, they'd deny it.

Instead, today, they want to discuss a related topic, but not that.

"We want to talk to you about seed," one of them said. "You have a separator, don't you?"

The farmer stared. They seemed to know a lot about him! Yes, it was true. He had such a machine.

"It's very old," the first one went on. "Victorian, wouldn't you say?"

"It still does the job."

"Yes, that's the point. You put aside some of your crop, run it through the machine and save the seed. You also do this service for some of your neighbours. Well, once our planting is established, you will have to stop. Permanently."

MacLawn was flabbergasted. He just stood there with his mouth open. He wouldn't be able to save his own seed?

"You won't," the second man agreed. "Not any more. From now on, you buy seed from us. Our company. Only."

"I don't understand."

The men leaned on the car. It was a cold day, but they seemed comfortable. They must have had this conversation many times, with farmers, at the sides of roads, maybe inside barns. It was a set speech, and they were running through it.

"We have the patent on the seed we are using on the field there," one of the legal people told the farmer. "If you plant your own seed, we will take you to court and accuse you of infringing our copyrights."

There was silence. MacLawn, for once in his life, had no idea what these men were saying.

"Is that legal?" he asked slowly. "Will it stand up in court?"

The lawyers chuckled, amused at some little in-joke between themselves.

"It's worked in America," they told him. "But then, the judges can be a lot more accommodating over there."

That's not the point, they told him. It doesn't matter whether they win or not, they could afford to fund a long-term litigation and he would probably be bankrupt before a verdict was even delivered. That was their strategy, how they worked.

MacLawn thought for a moment, then made up his mind. There was only one answer, then.

"The machine's in the barn," he said wearily. "Perhaps you need to see it, make sure it's what you think it is."

They nodded, thinking they had the farmer on the run, or maybe boxed into a corner. Either way, they had delivered the message and intimidated him sufficiently. It was all part of long-term plans for Barton Moss. He was just one farmer, after all.

They accompanied him into the barn, and Farmer MacLawn closed the door behind them.

When he came out, twenty minutes later, he had some parts in his hand and a screwdriver.

He went over to the men's car and started unscrewing the number plate. He put on the number plates he had taken from one of his vehicles. His car was about the same size and colour, so wouldn't be noticed if there was some kind of automatic check.

He would drive their car to a friend of his in Warrington, who had a garage that re-registered, re-painted and sold on stolen cars. The man would do his pal MacLawn a favour, no questions asked. The car, once a different colour, would effectively disappear.

As for the two men, they would never be seen again.

There was no CCTV this far out of town, so there was no evidence they came to MacLawn's farm or went somewhere else. They might be looked for, but they wouldn't be found. The search would be fruitless.

MacLawn sighed. They should have known about him, his past. What he did.

He hadn't always been a farmer.

The next day, Mickey went to visit Dr Jenner's house.

He'd had permission from the family. They'd all moved out, apparently, and were staying with relatives. The plan was to sell the house. It was big, worth quite a lot, and the Doctor's survivors would need cash now his income was lost to them.

They'd offered to give him a key, but Mickey knew he could manage. He took Terry with him, and the technician opened the door in seconds. Disabled the burglar alarm too. He was clever like that. He could do that sort of thing.

"What are we looking for?" Terry asked, looking around at the disorganised mess that scientists lived in.

There were papers everywhere, on shelves, on cupboards. The dining table was awash with reports, books, pamphlets. There were CD's in one corner, maybe DVD's too, and discs. There were laptops, many computers. Perhaps some of them belonged to the kids, but they were there and they'd all need examining. And more books.

Each room had bookshelves, even the kitchen.

"I don't know," Mickey admitted honestly.

The point was that something had got Jenner killed, and Mickey wondered if it would be obvious. Maybe some research the good Doctor had done recently. Some investigating into places he shouldn't have been.

The ideal clue would be a warning. If they found emails on his computer that said, 'Don't pursue this', or some anonymous letter, at least that would be something. After all, not everybody gets killed, especially scientists. There had to be a powerful reason.

Mickey looked around. It was a big house, maybe four bedrooms upstairs, but, looking at it, this seemed to be the place where the family did most of its living. It was a large through-lounge, with kitchen off to one side and access through a hatch for meals and refreshments to be sent in. There was a utility room behind that, maybe a back door.

Still, this would be the best place to start. Jenner clearly didn't have his own office in this place: he worked on the table.

Terry started on the bookshelves, pulling books out and looking behind them, as though he suspected a listening device, or a bug. He didn't find one. Then he started opening books, as if he thought they might be concealing things, like USB's. But No, no suspicious memory sticks, codes or keys. He seemed a little frustrated.

Then he pulled a device from his pocket. It

was about the size and shape of a TV remote control. He switched it on and started waving it around the room. It beeped once or twice, and he followed the direction, but again, found nothing.

Then Terry bent down and looked at the television, which wasn't as big as most houses had these days, and was on an old-fashioned table, in the corner of the room. It was as though he noticed something about it, something odd.

Mickey walked past him and came to large French windows, which were there to open, presumably, onto the extensive lawn and flower beds outside. It was a lovely house, and should fetch good money, now that the housing market was looking up again.

There was a low shed at the end of the garden, with a painted top. Mickey stared at it for several moments before realising what it truly was: it was a canal boat. Of course! One reason the house was so desirable was that it backed onto a canal, and they had their own mooring. So, the Doctor and family had their own boat too. They were very lucky.

Mickey tried the door handle, but the French windows were locked. He thought about asking Terry to pick them open, whenever he finished with that TV set that he was fiddling with. He'd like to have a look outside. It was cold, but there was a weak sun shining on the trees, with leaves turning gold and brown already, at last, since it was a late autumn.

Then something struck Mickey, an idea

popping into his head, quite forcibly.

He reached into his pocket and brought out a piece of paper. It was a map, the map that Jenner had given him, all those days ago. In the cafe, the Doctor had handed it over, saying that it showed where 'treasure' was buried. Mickey stared at the symbols. Suddenly, they made sense. There was a circle - that was the house. Round blobs and squares - the trees and planting. And there, along the top of the picture, something like a cylinder, with wavy lines. The canal!

Mickey followed the dots to the cross in the top right hand corner. That's where the stash is buried, he was thinking.

He got Terry to open the door and they burst out onto the lawn. They walked towards the water.

"You found something?" Mickey asked idly. He wasn't thinking about it, really. He was looking up to the right.

"I'll tell you later," Terry told him, "when I've run some tests."

Mickey reached the canal bank. The waterway was about three metres wide at this point, the banks supported by steel planking, the grass growing up to it neatly trimmed. There were houses to right and left of him, all along this side, and opposite, a towpath with hedges behind, and fields beyond that. It was a superb view. So rural. There were hills in the dim distance.

"I'd love to live here," he told Terry, as he

saw the water ripple in the wind and listened to the gentle lap of small waves.

"They've sunk his boat," Terry said quietly.

Mickey turned, shocked. It was true: the canal boat was a full-size steel-bottomed craft, maybe twenty metres long, gaily painted in the old style. It wasn't clear with a casual look, but it was low in the water. Mickey could now see, through the curtained windows, that there was water inside the boat, up to seat and bed level. Someone had scuppered it.

"Thorough," Terry commented.

CHAPTER FIVE: Fresh air

Mr Marks was fuming. He felt boxed in, imprisoned. The long days in the Safe House were getting to him.

"I need time out," he told his captors. "Get me out of here. I need fresh air."

As it happened, Mickey was there. It was his turn. He knew he hadn't been doing as many shifts as he could, so he was trying to make up for it. It was just his luck that this was the time their guest decided to kick off big time.

The problem was, it was early evening. Maybe they could go out for dinner, Mickey was thinking. But no, Mr Marks wanted to get out and about. But it was a cold, November evening in Manchester. It wasn't an appropriate time to stroll along the boulevard, or wander around the grassy verges of Piccadilly Gardens. Mickey looked at his fellow operatives: any ideas?

Then his phone buzzed. Mickey took it out of his pocket. Was this divine intervention? Guidance from the Gods?

It was Liv. The message was that Melia was going into the city that night to a lecture.

The implication was obvious. Mickey and Melia needed to talk, and if he wanted to find her, he could go to Methodist Hall on Oldham Street that very night and find her there. They had things to discuss, big things. Liv was trying to help.

Mickey gave a hearty vote of thanks. Sure, he needed to see Melia, and No, they hadn't even started debating the news in her life, and what it might mean to the both of them. But he was working - Okay, he would combine duties.

"Let's go out," he suggested. "Central Manchester. I'm sure we can find something interesting to do."

They were in the suburbs. Marks wanted a walk? Okay, they could leave the car in the drive and walk off down the road. That good enough for you? They strolled along the leafy avenue, turned the corner, walked past the park and school.

Within minutes they had reached the tram stop. What better? A tram ride into Manchester, the city centre.

It dropped them off at Piccadilly Gardens. Mickey led the way, walking them around and across, to Oldham Street.

The good thing, he was thinking, was that it was such an unexpected route, that if anybody had been detailed to follow them, then the pursuers would have stood out. But they didn't see anyone, not in the street, on the tram, or in the Gardens.

Mickey walked Mr Marks and his other two escorts past the shops and bars and stopped on the steps of the Hall.

"What do you know?" he said brightly. "There's a lecture on tonight, on the works of Ken Wilber."

Mr Marks, Wilkins and Mickey had no idea who that was or why they were important. But the fourth member of the party, a young woman called Sillence, perked up. She'd read some of his books, she said. Yay, that would be interesting.

She said: "It's all about the difference between 'Waking Up' and "Growing Up'. You know, we all look for Enlightenment - "

"Whoah," Marks said sarcastically. "Don't spoil it for me."

Ms Sillence gave a small smile. You're a ruthless businessman, she was thinking. This is exactly what you need.

It was a big building, with many rooms on many floors, and there were a number of activities going on that night, meetings and talks. Even a choir rehearsal, it said on the board near the entrance. Mickey spotted the sign for the Wilber lecture and led them up the stairs to one of the main rooms. It was round, with a table at the front and rows of chairs arranged in a semi-circle.

Melia was already there, over to the right. Mickey kept to the left and pointed at chairs near the back. His gang obliged and took their places. It was near a door, Mickey pointed out to Wilkins; it might be needed if there was an emergency.

Mickey stood against the wall for a moment, looking round. There were all sorts of people filing in, old and young, male and female. None of them looked like a paid assassin. Not yet.

He looked at the back of Melia's head. She wasn't alone. She was sitting next to a young man, and Mickey could tell they were together because they kept leaning in towards each other to talk and chat. They seemed quite close.

He had no idea who this person was, and it gave him a little twinkle of jealousy. It was another man. What did it mean?

There was a burst of spontaneous applause as several important looking people came in and made their way to the front. There was some negotiation as they sorted themselves out, then they sat in a row along the table, like a 'Brains' Trust'.

One woman, dressed in rugs and scarves, got to her feet and commandeered the microphone. Mickey sat down.

None of them were Ken Wilber. He was in America, writing more books. But these people were all his supporters, followers and acolytes. They would each take an aspect of his work and introduce it. Then there would be a general discussion, with the audience invited to contribute.

Mickey smiled. It sounded thrilling, he was thinking.

"We are all seeking Enlightenment - " the woman said, kicking things off.

Yes, Mickey was thinking, I've heard that.

He looked along the line at the young agent called Sillence. She was leaning forward in her chair, rapt. Well, that wouldn't do; if she wasn't paying attention to the job in hand, keeping an eye on Marks, then Mickey was going to have to do it himself.

He raised his head, looked around, and kept an eye on the crowd. So far, there didn't seem anyone interested in them.

Okay, what was the message? We all seek Enlightenment, and generally we think that's going to come abruptly, in a flash of light, the woman said. We practise various modalities, like Yoga, or Meditation, or physical interventions like massage or reiki, but still, we imagine it's all building up to some grand divine revelation – and, if it arrives and we have that, we're perfect.

Ken Wilber had a different idea. It's not about 'Waking Up', he said. You need to think about progress as 'Growing Up'. That means several things; it means that as you explore philosophies and ways of seeing the world, you are learning all the time, and that's good. You don't need some blockbuster moment at the end of it all - you're getting better at each step along the way. Also, you don't have to imagine that all the years of trying are merely the steps to climbing up the mountain, and thinking you're not really getting anywhere until you've got to the top. No. Each footfall is making you a better person, and should be valued. And every place you are should be valued. Don't devalue what you're doing, learning or attempting because you haven't made the expected breakthrough. Instead, appreciate each moment along your journey and enjoy the scenery. It's all beautiful.

Well, that's Good News, Mickey was thinking. I've not such a slob as I thought. I'm learning on my 'journey', after all.

He looked over to see what effect this was having on Melia. Her head was down, and as she turned slightly to one side to wipe away a tear, he saw quite clearly that she was crying. Oh dear, Mickey thought. I'm not there. I'm here.

He stood up, excusing himself, then pushed his way along the line of people and chairs until he was over by the wall on the right of the room. He walked down towards the front and slipped into the row behind Melia. He had some idea he could hold her hand. All the chairs were occupied either side of her, and he would have liked to sit beside her, but that wasn't possible.

The first speaker finished, there was applause and she handed the microphone to the person next to her.

In the changeover, the audience took the opportunity to cough a little, and comment to their friends. Some moved around.

Mickey hardly saw what happened, but suddenly there were two angry men standing in front of Melia, glaring at her.

She drew back. She recognised them. The last time she had seen them was at Manchester Hospital, when Terry had chased them away. She looked around in panic, but there was no Terry nearby. She felt alone and threatened.

Then something strange happened. Snopes,

who was sitting beside her, leapt to his feet and charged at the men with his arms outstretched. He was like a human hurricane. He just swept them off their feet and clattered them into the table behind them.

But that time, Mickey had leapt out of his seat, jumped over Snopes's empty chair in one bound and landed on the men, pinning them to the floor. The man who had inherited the microphone was screaming and calling for order, but this wasn't a general riot, and most people remained where they were, unmotivated and unmoved. Only Mickey's team reacted, hurtling out of their chairs at speeds that only trained operatives could reach. They carried handcuffs. In seconds they had pinioned the attackers' hands behind them, dragged them to their feet and were bustling them towards the nearest door, out of the hall and into the corridor outside. The people at the table looked completely shocked, and were unable to react.

This is just a hurdle on your journey, Mickey wanted to tell them. Just clamber over it and move on.

He took Melia's arm, tenderly, and led her outside. She was shaking. It wasn't like her. She was usually tougher than that.

Outside, with the door shut behind them, they made a strange tableaux. Wilkins and Sillence hanging on to two bad guys, handcuffed and dazed. Mickey and Melia propping each other up, and Snopes, standing back, looking sheepish.

Melia looked at him and realised she hadn't introduced her date for the night.

"This is Snoopy's cousin," she said to the team.

Mickey was about to say something, but then a door opened, further along the corridor. It was one of the doors at the back of the hall, level with where they had all been sitting earlier. Mr Marks, bored and abandoned, decided he didn't want to be left alone. He came out to see what was going on. When he saw the people, the little crowd, he simply looked ungrateful, as if he thought they were having a better time than he was.

Behind him, the corridor led on, around the building, and Mickey could clearly see a staircase, one of the many.

As he focused on Marks, wondering what to tell him and how they would look after him from now on, now that they had these prisoners to process, Mickey was shocked to see another couple of guys in suits appear at the top of the stairs. They looked sinister. Mickey didn't know why, but he dropped Melia's hand, readying himself for action. He moved forward.

Sure enough, the guys spotted Mr Marks and approached him. He wasn't looking their way, so one of them seemed to decide to grab one of the Marks's arms, which spun him round to face them. He stepped back, suddenly fearful. He raised his hands in front of his face.

Mickey was convinced he heard Marks say, 'You! Why you?', but then he was pressed back against the door.

The team weren't about to let Mickey face an attack on his own. As trained WSB agents they knew how to defend each other, and how to assault others. Wilkins went left, Sillence went right. As Mickey closed on the new arrivals, the trio brought their fists to bear together, in unison. Mickey had a good grip on one guy and pulled him away from Marks and towards him. Mickey felt a hand whistle by his shoulder. He half turned and saw Melia by his side. He grinned. That's where he wanted her.

It wasn't a fight, it was a rout. The Unit, four of them, outnumbered and outfought the new arrivals. They pinned them to the floor and removed the threat to Mr Marks. Unfortunately, they had used up their supply of handcuffs, but Sillence found some rope on the back of a door marked 'Store' and applied it to the situation. She sat on the back of one man and reached for her phone. They would need Back-Up, she told the hotline at Regional Office. Send a van. Four prisoners.

At that precise moment, as if more support was needed, Dolf came walking up the same stairs. He wasn't alone.

"What are you doing here?" Mickey demanded, knowing that he couldn't have simply reacted to the call.

Dolf looked confused. "I'm bringing my wife

to a concert," he said.

That wasn't quite true. Regional Office made a point of keeping track of its staff, so there was a note on the Main Board that Mickey and others were in Methodist Hall. There was a concert on there, Dolf knew that, but he also thought it would be prudent to be in the same building, just in case he was needed. Looking at the trussed-up pair, he realised he wasn't.

"Let me introduce Kiko," he said to his colleagues. Melia shook her hand, pleased to meet another woman.

She was Asian. It wasn't immediately clear from which country, but she smiled graciously, pleased to greet Dolf's work colleagues. She looked as though she would be happy to invite all of them over for supper, now that they knew she existed.

"You're like a breath of fresh air," Melia said, smiling hugely.

"Looks like you've been working hard," the girl said with a grin. She admired the team's fortitude, just as she admired Dolf.

Melia nodded. Four prisoners, she said. Yes, a good haul. A good night's work.

"Where are the other two?" Kiko asked politely.

She was looking over Melia's shoulder. All she could see was a body on the floor. That was Snopes. But no sign of any 'prisoners' there. Nobody trussed up or in handcuffs, for instance. Even if there had once been.

Melia hurried over, Mickey in pursuit. Yes, Snopes was on the floor, groaning. He didn't seem badly damaged, but he had been surprised, he said. They had bundled him out of the way, and made off. He pointed towards the other stairs, beyond him.

Mickey cursed. We shouldn't have left an amateur in charge, he was thinking. While he and his mates were tackling the new threat, they had forgotten about the last threat, thinking it was neutralised. Obviously, they weren't. They had recovered, and escaped.

Melia was sympathetic. It's not what he's used to, she told Mickey. Give him a break.

Mickey sighed. It wasn't a good time to get careless. As far as he could see there was an unending supply of pairs of rough men in smart suits, ready to do damage, or maybe even kidnap, people associated with Crapanza, and all its history.

The only thing that was slightly confusing was that these assorted soldiers actually seemed to be mercenaries, working both sides. After all, some had been sent to take care of Jenner, but he was against a lot of what the chemical company was doing. Now, only a few weeks later, there were people after Marks, and he was a company man, right up there in the hierarchy.

Were the attackers directly employed by anybody? If not, how were Mickey and the team going to stop them?

Melia coughed and looked unwell. She

gazed around for a toilet and rushed towards it. It was a small door with a 'Disabled' sign on the door. That was all right, she was thinking. Right at that moment she felt completely incapacitated.

Mickey didn't know whether to follow, for support, or give her space, if she needed privacy. Luckily, she left the door open, so that gave him permission to hang around, discourage anyone coming in and protect her, but still give her distance.

She was leaning over the sink, but Mickey wasn't sure if she was being sick or not. She seemed to be crying.

"Liv told me you'd be here," he said gently, quietly, so no one else could hear.

Melia straightened up. "Well, I'm glad someone is thinking clearly," she said.

Mickey stopped. He didn't know what she meant, or what she would say next.

"It's simple," Melia told him. "I'm going to have a baby and it's going to change my life forever. I want to know where you are."

"Is it mine?" Mickey blurted out, unable to prevent saying the one thing he had been thinking all along.

"Would it matter?"

Mickey was silent. He could hardly put into words the agony he was going through.

Yes, maybe it would. I mean, he was thinking, he hardly had any claim on Melia. They had been 'going out' for many years, but it was an on/off relationship, and there was an understanding that they might find someone else, both of them. If Melia had got herself a new boyfriend, Mickey was thinking, I'd have no right to stand in the way of her settling for him.

But I'd hate it, he realised. Yes, he did love Melia - he'd been made aware of that several years ago - and he'd always imagined they could make a life together, like in the same house, at the same time. He just didn't know when that would be. If it was now - he could adjust to that, willingly. Well, not in his new place, he was thinking, and not with him moving into her long established city centre flat. They'd have to start somewhere else, somewhere new. Somewhere - Heaven forbid - in the suburbs.

They could do that. He could support her - he had his Army pension and his part-time earnings. They both might have to give up roaming the wild world and being secret agents, even if for only a few years.

Someone would have to stay home and mind the baby.

Mickey looked around. I guess this is the way my life has been, unexpected and unpredictable. I never thought I would be having intense discussions and making life-changing decisions in a church's Disabled toilet.

Then another thought occurred to him: did Snopes let the bad guys go?

He had captured them, after all, and that was very unexpected. Maybe too unexpected. What if it had been a set-up? Something to make the young man look good but not a serious threat. Mickey didn't know the guy well enough to judge.

"When you've finished debating our future in your head," Melia said testily, "maybe you'll share your thoughts with me."

Mickey grimaced. Yes, he had been thinking about them and 'their future', but then he hadn't. That was him. He would never cease being an investigator and an action man, even if he took a career break.

"My thought," Mickey said, "is that you and me could take time off, spend a day together and get to grips with it all."

Melia turned. Her face was smeared, but she looked good enough to eat, Mickey was thinking. She always would.

"Give me five minutes alone," she asked him. "Then get your diary out."

Mickey backed up and closed the door, allowing her peace.

Gibson was standing in front of him.

The boss was here? Following Marks - or someone else? Was there anything else going on?

"I'm here for the Powerhouse meeting," he said, confirming it. "I didn't expect to see the whole of my squad on duty!"

In a few quick sentences Mickey outlined how he, Wilkins and Sillence had brought Marks into town for a quiet night off. Then they met Melia and her new friend, a Mr Snopes, and things had developed. He also mentioned Dolf, (but not his new bride).

The Captain was quiet. He took several deep breaths. He seemed to be worried about one thing in particular.

"Is this 'Snopes' the same as our Mr Snopes?" he asked at last. He seemed moved.

Mickey confirmed what he had so recently been told: same family.

Gibson stood a little more upright. "We do whatever we can for him," he instructed Mickey. In honour of Snoopy.

Mickey made a sour face. Yeah, well, this Mr Snopes didn't look as if he needed anyone else's help.

"I'm here," the Captain said, searching for words, "because the new government has seen fit to continue the last Chancellor of the Exchequer's plan to develop business and infrastructure across the north of England. from Liverpool to Hull."

Mickey nodded. He'd read about some of the proposals. It was obvious they'd want someone from WSB there, to consider the security implications. No wonder they had sent for the top man.

Gibson said: "I don't want to go back in that room and tell the people there that we are being compromised in this very building, and that there are thugs running around now, this evening, beyond our ability to restrain and detain them."

A shot rang out.

It was as much a surprise to Mickey as anyone. He turned and was concerned to see the girl Sillence come bounding up the far staircase, looking for help. She stared around wildly, spotted Mickey and the boss, and hurried over.

"Wilkins has been shot," she reported. She didn't say anymore. She seemed lost for words.

Mr Marks came out from the main room again, where he had gone, preferring the discussion there to the one in the corridor. He walked over towards Mickey, looking grim. He didn't seem impressed either.

"Thank goodness my men are here," he told Gibson. "I think I can rely on my assistant, at least."

You can rely on us, the Captain wanted to reassure him, but his heart wasn't in it.

Mickey's phone buzzed. He looked down at the message. It said, 'Second floor, back' and was signed 'Dolf'.

A few minutes later, Mickey and Melia were scouring the next floor down, looking for Dolf.

They found him in the corridor. He was on one knee, examining two bodies on the floor. Everyone present started off assuming that they were the pair who had 'escaped' from Snopes earlier.

But they weren't. Whatever had happened to those two wasn't at that moment clear. But this was a new pair of baddies, and whatever their mission – Well, it hadn't got very far.

Dolf, noting the new faces and the mortal wounds, was clearly annoyed, not least because he had arrived too late, and alone.

"These men have been executed," he said to his team-mates. He looked disgusted.

"I think you will find," a voice said quietly, "that they were killed in self-defence."

Everyone turned around. Mr Marks was standing there and, next to him, a swarthy man in a purple suit. He looked American.

Marks said: "This is my assistant, Mr Bartoli. He is licensed to carry a gun, and he has dealt with these attackers."

Rather more definitively that we are used to, Mickey wanted to say, but didn't. He couldn't afford to upset Mr Marks.

Mickey took Melia's arm and led her back down the corridor. He wasn't sure why, but he had moved into protective mode.

The corridor exploded with action as local police arrived, surrounding everyone, taking names, taping off areas. It was good that Mickey and Melia weren't right on top of the crime scene. Dolf was still there and he was being questioned aggressively.

Mr Marks, having established his credentials, was allowed to go back upstairs.

Then Terry appeared, looking harassed, as usual. He didn't have his usual kitbag with him.

"Thank goodness," Mickey told him. "You'll need to record the area before they ruin it for evidence."

Terry snorted. "I'm not here for crime, not that sort of crime, anyway. I've come to see you."

He stood right in front of Mickey,

confronting him, even though he was a good deal shorter.

Terry said: "Mickey, you're going to have to live with reality. There's every reason to believe that the child Melia is carrying belongs to me. You were away, we were together for a while. We're both adults. It happened. Maybe I'm a Dad, at last."

Mickey took a deep breath, uncertain what to say, and how to say it. He let the words sink in for a few moments.

Then he asked the technician: "And will you be taking responsibility? Are you saying that you and Melia will be living together?"

"That can't happen, I'm afraid. It was some time ago and we've all moved on. No, if you wish to step back into Melia's life and take up where your relationship left off, then that's fine by me. That's what I came here to tell you. The sooner you know, the better. Just work it out between you two. I wish you well. If there is to be a wedding, I'd be honoured to be a guest."

Blimey, Mickey was thinking, I hadn't even considered that!

Slowly he said: "And you are in a new relationship?"

"I'm with Liv now," Terry told him.

As for Liv, she had gone to see her grandfather.

It was the question of autism that had brought her there. She wanted to know if there was a history in the family. She couldn't ask her Dad, he was dead, so she thought of asking her Dad's Dad. That's as close to information as she was going to get.

She hadn't been looking forward to it. Her granddad lived in Irlam, on the edge of Barton Moss, in one of the old Council houses that had been built in the previously rural area in the 1960s. It was a 'green field' site, and she remembered how much her Dad had enjoyed his childhood, running out in the fields and woods, playing along the hedges and down into the streams.

It was a strange site. There was a row of houses and the back gardens led directly onto farmland. It was abrupt, immediate. It was as though the houses were dropped into the middle of the countryside, but all around them, it stayed the same.

The strangest thing was the street lamps. The road had them, and you could see your way to the houses, but behind the houses, it was totally black. It was truly the edge of darkness. It was spooky. Liv could remember visiting the property, but it was years ago, when her granddad was hale and hearty and still speaking to her Dad. Then they fell out, a family rift developed that was not even healed enough for her gran and granddad to come to her Dad's funeral. They didn't show.

When she knocked on the door she was expecting to be rebuffed, but her granddad just grunted and led her into the kitchen. He put the kettle on and started making tea, as if twenty years hadn't really come and gone, and now never existed.

"How's my Gran?" Liv asked, but the old man just grunted at that too.

He didn't seem concerned with anything, not bothered by daily problems or issues. He started coughing.

"That sounds bad," Liv said. "You've been to the Doctor?"

He shook his head. Why bother, was his attitude. He was old and there wasn't much that doctors could do for him.

"They've been spraying again," he said, as if that explained everything. He pointed to a leaflet on the windowsill.

It was a glossy and colourful page. The headline said: 'Why you don't have to worry about pesticides'. That was an odd thing to send information out about, but yes, all the neighbours had received it, the old man said.

"Your Gran has taken it bad," he said. "But then, she's always had a bad chest."

Liv shook her head. She had no memory of that. Her Grandma had been a large and impressive lady, as she recalled. Very forthright, everyone said. Not afraid to speak her own mind. Always sticking up for the little people.

Liv loved her.

They took their cups into the living room. The telly was turned on but the sound was down.

It was dark, a badly-lit place.

"Gran?"

The old lady was slumped in an easy chair, a blanket around her shoulders and her hair covering her face. She looked collapsed in on herself, far shorter and smaller than Liv could ever recall. She didn't look up, didn't acknowledge Liv.

"She gets like that," Granddad said. "She's been very quiet these last few weeks, since the helicopters came over."

Liv put her cup down on the side and went over to her gran. She put a hand on her head, smoothing down her curls. The hair seemed cold. That didn't feel right. Liv moved closer, bending over, getting to the old lady's level.

She was wearing an old dress, faded and very worn. It came up to her neck, but her neck was very scrawny and lined. It was also covered in blue marks. Bruises. Liv followed the skin down and pushed the dress a little way along her gran's shoulders.

There were more blue marks. Bruises? Red wheals too, ugly marks.

Panicking, Liv looked further down. Was her gran breathing? Yes, but it was shallow, almost non-existent.

"She's not her usual self," Liv's granddad said. "Usually we have a bit of banter. But she doesn't have the energy she used to have, and she gets so uppity. Keeps telling me there's something wrong with the water. She won't drink her tea. Makes me mad."

Liv looked at him and saw an ageing, frail man, lost in a make-believe world, completely cut off from reality.

"We need to get this woman to hospital," Liv declared, nearly shouting.

Her granddad didn't reply. He said not a word.

CHAPTER SIX: Fresh food

A few days later, Mr Marks got to have another outing.

This time it was business, not pleasure.

One of the things he had been tasked by his employers to do, while in Britain, was to initiate, delegate and finalise arrangements for the launch of the Sugar Pipeline, bringing natural sweeteners into this country from the USA. Salford's Mayor would be there.

The title, of course, was completely misleading. It wasn't sugar, it was Corn Syrup, and it wasn't a pipeline.

It was an ocean-going tanker.

One advantage that Manchester had over many of its rival industrial cities in the north of England, was that it had its own connection to the sea - the Manchester Ship Canal. The waterway had become a little rundown in recent years, and the docks at Salford were now finding other uses, such as being the new location for TV and radio studios for the BBC. But the link was still there, and the new owners of the facilities saw its potential, and the opportunity to work with chemical companies like Crapanza.

Mr Marks was invited to the Headquarters of the Corsh Corporation, on the banks of what had once been called the River Irwell, and with light-bulbs popping, he sat at a table and signed an impressive looking contract. That was Phase

One.

The next phase was actually to wait on the banks and watch as the first tanker docked.

No expense had been spared. The new dock was further downriver from central Salford at Irlam, next to the new container port. A stand had been erected for important people to sit in, and flags and banners were strung up. Music was playing. The BBC Philharmonic were there.

A huge screen at the side of the stand showed live pictures, taken by the company's drones. At that precise moment, it showed a tanker steaming sedately up the canal from the sea. It had the recognisable logo of Crapanza on its side.

Mr Marks wasn't happy.

"Where are my usual bodyguards?" he complained to Captain Gibson.

The boss of WSB, splendidly dressed and turned out for the day, didn't want to admit the fact that he didn't know. But the simple truth was that Mickey and Melia kept phoning in sick, and he was left with the B team to do their work.

Dolf was there, plus Sillence, and the young tyke Wilkins, who was out of the hospital and determined not to let a small bullet hole in his bicep and his arm in a sling deter him from doing his job. The Captain indulged his enthusiasm and let him work, even though he would be completely useless in a crisis. There were others, Gibson reasoned.

Actually, the Captain was less than happy to

be dragged out of his office for a dismal and cold day in November, with the wind whipping off the water of the Canal, but this was an event that had been discussed at the Powerhouse meeting. The new dock facilities were seen as a bold step in improving infrastructure in the Northern Corridor and, coincidentally, Corsh Inc. were also involved in improving docks at Liverpool and Hull. They had to be supported, everyone agreed.

Then there were the demonstrators.

It seemed that not everyone in this part of the world were thrilled by the kind of food products that were being shipped. Some Bolsheviks were saying that Corn Syrup was equivalent to a poison, with its effect on the bodies of its consumers. That seemed a little unfair, even Gibson had concluded. Sure, there was a outbreak of the plague of obesity in this area, but almost certainly that was due to the overindulgence of the population, wasn't it? People were eating too much these days, bigger portions and faster food. You couldn't blame that on Crapanza, could you? The fact that they, as food processors as well as suppliers, put corn syrup in just about every single one of their products, from bread to ready meals, wasn't to blame, was it?

Questions were not Captain Gibson's favourites. He preferred answers. Since so much of the controversy surrounding Mr Marks and his company was unproven, it merely made him nervous. He found such discussions too 'political' for his taste.

He turned to his assistant, Terry, who was carrying a small tablet computer. The Captain raised his eyebrows in a question. Terry nodded. All under control, he seemed to be saying. Everyone is in place and ready.

They would need to be. The placard-waving rabble-rousers, with their 'No more Frankenstein-foods' message, were singing and shouting, and appeared to be on the edge of hysteria. WSB didn't want that bubbling over.

The company wasn't about to let a gaggle of unwashed students interfere with its master-plan.

They decided to start with the speeches.

The elected Mayor of Salford, Sol Senate, was first up to the platform. He was a young, energetic politician, who was anxious to promote everything that brought glory and notice to his adopted city. He was keen for this new investment, he said, and was looking forward to the jobs that the dock and transit links would make. He shouted into the microphone and temporarily drowned out the socialists behind the fence. Once, of course, when only slightly younger, he would have been amongst them, rather than enjoying the present day trappings of elected office.

A genial weatherman from the commercial TV company came up onto the stage. He had been appointed the Master of Ceremonies for the event, paid by the food processors. He consulted the clipboard in his hand. Mrs Jenner was next.

"Mrs Jenner?" he called. "Is Mrs Jenner here? Ready?"

Gibson looked frosty, but Marks tried to calm him. Yes, it had been his idea, he said. Don't forget, Jenner had done a lot of good work for the company before he went rogue. Mr Marks thought his widow might have some kind words for the people paying her pension. It seemed like a good idea at the time, he said. Like building bridges.

Still, she didn't appear, so the MC brought on the local Primary School choir. That was a good idea, everyone loved kids.

But not teenagers. A whole bunch of students, taking a day off from their studies in Manchester, were chanting over by a fence at the side of the site. They must have leaned too heavily on the wire, because it suddenly gave way.

"Protect my property!" Marks demanded. Gibson, on behalf of WSB, looked unimpressed, but he asked Dolf to go and talk to them. As the nearest thing to a 'young person' in the team, his boss thought Dolf might be able to speak their language.

That challenge was superseded. There was the sound of revving engines, like motorbikes, but it was nothing on land. It was the sound of outboard engines. From nowhere, a pair of rubber dinghies appeared on the river, and started racing backwards and forwards, churning up the water and making a tremendous racket. The school choir became inaudible.

Just at that moment, the tanker hove into view, coming around the bend.

The small boats, spotting their target, speeded towards it, then started running rings around it.

They were squaring up for a confrontation.

Gibson wasn't about to be defeated. He pulled out his phone and got on to the Deputy Chief Constable, whom he kept on Speed Dial. He asked for the police helicopter, and for the frogmen team, just in case.

Meanwhile, Dolf was in front of a line of police dogs, trying to talk moderation to the protestors. With placards saying things like, 'Poisoners', 'Animal murderers', 'Crap causes Autism' and 'Where does infertility come from?', it might have seemed like a lost cause. Dolf didn't give up. They're not going to fade away, he was thinking. We have to find a way to contain them.

The speedboats were far worse of a problem.

The ship's captain knew that he had to bring the big ship smoothly into a berth alongside the river. They would tie up and unloading tubes would be lowered into his holds and pumping would commence. He had done it dozens of times, not here of course, but at other ports around the world. He was experienced. An old sea dog.

Still, the River Irwell, even though canalised, straightened and renamed as the Manchester Ship Canal, was unfamiliar to him. It made him uncertain and indecisive. The little craft reminded him of the Greenpeace boats that harassed whaling ships. He knew that always led to trouble, but he had never had to deal with such intimidation. He slowed the engines, trying to avoid them.

A worse problem for him was that he was confused by the new Container Port. That was an inlet off the river. He could see that, and the cranes and railway tracks beyond. He knew from the charts supplied to him, and the written instructions, that he had to ignore the new dock and moor up parallel to the river, it simply didn't look right. There were no other big ships around. Yet.

Standing in the bridge, at the top of the big tanker, it was hard to get a good view down to the water, and the fast little dinghies were running around his ship at random. He was inclined to simply ignore them, but then he heard a shout from a man watching the nearside that there was a speedboat between them and the landing, and he panicked, increasing engine thrust and moving back out into the main stream. The ship veered uncertainly.

"Hard astern!" he commanded, wanting to lose speed. At this rate of knots, they would overshoot the berth and cut across the entrance to the container dock. He didn't want that. The man on the helm turned the wheel, obeying orders.

The tanker simply couldn't turn fast enough. The bow of the ship started turning, back towards the bank, but they were still moving forward. The prow slammed into the very corner of the dock, bouncing off the rubber tyres and struts that supported the quay, and sliding back across the river. The little boats were nearly swamped, right then and there.

"Starboard," the captain shouted, but it was already too late. The strain on the ship had compromised its balance.

Gibson, standing at the top of the platform on the bank, was astonished to see the tanker slowly keel over, lying, as it did, right across the river. It toppled elegantly onto its side, completely blocking all navigation.

He was reminded of what 'Unsinkable' Molly Brown had said, when she was sitting in a lifeboat watched the Titanic slide under the waves: "Now that's a sight you don't see every day." He agreed. He shook his head in disbelief.

The police helicopter arrived and hovered over the disaster, its downdraught stirring up the water. The speedboats had been overcome with water, one turned over and one disappeared completely. There were people wearing life jackets in the river.

Over on the stage, the performers had been stunned into silence. The choir had trailed off and everyone stood, wondering what to do. Nobody knew what would happen next. Then sirens split the air. Police and ambulances were on their way.

Dolf, down at ground level, didn't have a good view, but he noted that the protestors nearest the water were all turned in that direction, looking at something. They had stopped chanting, stopped waving their placards aggressively. They were standing, looking out at the capsized craft, with a strange, 'We never meant that to happen' look on their faces.

Then they started shouting again, looking at each other, enraged by some new development.

Gibson, from his eyrie, could see the problem.

Which was a glutinous yellow stain spreading out into the water. The tanker was leaking. Some pipe or tank had sprung a break and corn syrup was getting out, and was busy washing away, diluted but still a threat.

The protestors went wild. They had arrived, thinking they were there to stop food additives arriving that would compromise the health of the nation, and now they were witnessing the biggest spillage the River Irwell had seen since the 1920s.

They were livid. Pollution was a worse sin than poison!

Those poor fish.

Thinking about the Jenners, Mickey decided to go and visit the family in their new home.

He had only been given hazy information about Dr Jenner's relatives, and wasn't sure who he would meet. The person who opened the door was a young lady, very well dressed and together. She introduced herself as the elder daughter, recently left University and starting out on a career in the Law. A slight change from the Jenner tradition of involvement in Science.

They were joined in the hallway by a young man, who said he was the son. He was informally dressed, with a sweatshirt advertising his membership of a University football team. He also rowed, he said.

It was a small house, maybe two bedrooms. Mickey could see that he door on the right led to a lounge, and the door on the left led to a kitchen and dining area. The stairs were in front of them.

Well, he was thinking, if Mrs Jenner had sold her old house, the family would come out ahead, probably with a hefty wedge of cash. That could be handy, now that the main wage-earner was gone.

Mickey thought it would be awkward when he explained who he was, but the kids seemed pleased to meet him. He was the last person to see their father alive and they said they would like to hear all about the incident. They seemed keen to hear the details of how their father died. He was some kind of hero to them, and they wanted to know he faced his fate bravely.

"Is your mother not at home?" Mickey asked politely.

A shadow fell across their faces.

"She died," the girl said quietly.

Mickey was shocked. Losing one parent is bad enough, but both of them? It was unthinkable.

He wanted to ask - but all they said was that it was some kind of traffic accident, and yes, it was sudden.

"What am I thinking?" the daughter said. "Come in the kitchen and I'll make you a cup of tea."

Then Mickey met the other visitor.

That was a shock too. As he walked in the kitchen area, he was surprised to see a man in a suit sitting at the dining table. He had papers in front of him and a laptop open. He looked like a lawyer. He smelt like a lawyer.

"This is Mr Bowbiss," the son said. "He's advising us."

The man stopped what he was doing, stood up and shook Mickey's hand. He had a damp handshake.

He didn't seem the slightest bit interested in who Mickey was, but he was willing to offer his details.

"I have been instructed by a firm called Sagar International. They are concerned about the way the family is being treated," he said.

By Crapanza. What have they done now? Mickey asked wearily. What outrage have the firm committed?

"They are contesting Dr Jenner's patent on Sucrosanct, the ubiquitous artificial sweetener that he invented."

Mickey took a breath. Wow, that seemed like a big deal.

From his brief talk to Jenner, Mickey got the

impression that was the one thing that the old man had seemed most proud of. He had come up with a totally new product, something that was now indispensable in the food industry. So, a compound worth millions.

Why were the bastards he used to work for trying to rob him of it, the one testament to his life's research?

"Nobody knows," the smart man said. "Who knows what goes through the minds of the executives in Switzerland?"

The fact remained: the family had received papers and the gist was that the firm were alleging that since the scientist had occasionally been employed by them whilst he was developing the new sweetener, the patent should belong to the company.

"It is strange that they haven't seen it like that until now," the man noted.

It was vindictive, almost like it was part of a campaign. The doctor was gone and now they were trying to erase all trace of him.

And yes, it was a big deal. The annual income from all the users, each one paying a small dividend for the privilege of putting the product into all the foods and derivatives they manufactured throughout the year, was worth a very hefty sum.

Can they do that? Mickey wanted to know. Can they take the patent from the Jenners?

"The way they work," the man said slowly, as if explaining to children, "is that they file suit and then challenge you to take them to court. They have the lawyers, you will have to hire some. The general strategy is to put you - the innocent party - in a position where you simply can't afford to fight the case. Then, they hope, you will settle, out of court."

"What would a settlement entail?" Mickey asked, understanding, despite the man's lack of confidence in him.

"Oh, probably a fairly large pot of cash. Yes, they will make it look as if they are being generous, and it will seem like an offer the family can't refuse. Still, it will be a fraction of the lifetime earnings from the product. Plus, they will then have control of the market, and they will squeeze the customers on price, as they always do. They are not principled, you must see that."

Mickey was learning.

He sat on a stool at the breakfast bar and watched the man at work, tapping on his laptop, scrutinising the correspondence from Crapanza. This was the bit he didn't understand, though: he knew that Sagar were a rival to the Crap team, so why would they get involved? Why were they on the side of the Jenners? What were they trying to prove?

What did they hope to gain?

Mickey accepted the offer of tea, then a cake, which the children managed to find in a cupboard. He talked to them while the man worked, told them everything he could about his encounter with their father and later, asked them questions.

The problem for Mickey was still there. Jenner had been killed by professionals, a pair of assassins in a pimped-up car, but there was no evidence who they were or who sent them. A casual member of the public, hearing of Dr Jenner's connection to certain ruthless companies in the fields of food and chemicals, might posit a link, and suppose that the bad guys in the industry had paid for the hit. But where was the proof? Where was the evidence? Mickey was floundering.

Still, because of the man he was and is, he wouldn't let it go.

I will find some facts. I will find some clues, he decided. I will hunt down the dogs who did this awful crime and then -

Well, then he would deal with them, as only he could.

Mickey looked at the man at the table. Not like him, he was thinking. Not with papers and writs.

I won't be suing anybody.

Later that day Terry paused for coffee and cake.

He'd done what he could at the scene near the Irlam Locks, but capsized ocean tankers weren't his speciality. He'd filmed it, and posted some pics on social media - under his own name and others - but that was as far as it went.

It was too 'real world' for his taste.

So he took his laptop and his bag and jumped on the nearest passing bus, going towards Manchester. Only a few minutes up the road he spotted shops, bars and restaurants and jumped out. He saw a little shop front: it said 'Tea Room'.

That was his style exactly - slightly old-fashioned and rustic. Despite his high-tech exterior, he loved Olde Worlde.

They asked him if he had a booking.

He baulked. That was a bit too 'traditional', even for him. Besides, he couldn't believe it. This place was that popular?

Indeed it was. They kept him waiting by the serving hatch until a young couple finished their vegetable soup, then they fitted him in. It was the window seat. He turned his chair so that he could ignore the passers-by, and opened his laptop.

Terry was a man in demand. People were always dropping in to his cubbyhole at Regional Office with things for him to do. But most of it was mundane, repetitive. It was too easy for a man of his training and experience.

So he printed up a sign that read: 'Turn it off and turn it on again' and pinned it to the front of his door. That would show them!

Thus, in the usual course of events, with this small window of time to himself, he would have looked at his spreadsheet and chosen the most challenging, or interesting, or 'impossible' task and do some work on that. That would be his choice.

But today was different. Now he had responsibilities. For the last couple of months he had Liv in his life, and she was steadily taking centre-stage in his every waking thought. His main aim in life had developed into a mission to keep her happy.

And alive.

He hated to admit it, but the 'research' that she was doing was attracting attention, and from all the wrong quarters.

She had started getting hate mail. And threats. Her social media presence was being trolled and her pictures were being tampered with and defaced. It was all getting ugly. Terry decided he needed to give the problem his attention and expertise.

A waitress came over, took his order and went away. While he was waiting for the goods to arrive, he played the internet.

The simplest method, he had always found, was to pretend to be the victim and see what he could provoke. That way he could examine the comments, then follow them back to their source. That was easy for him to do. Also, it was easy for him to sign on as Liv - she didn't have the greatest imagination in the realm of passwords - and he was able to log in and out at will.

He hadn't told her. He regretted that. If they were to have a life together, he knew he was going to have to be honest with her. But not yet. Let me solve this problem, he was thinking. Let me fight off this challenge, like a King of the

Jungle -

No, he wasn't a lion, he decided. More like one of the other big cats. Maybe a tiger, skulking through the jungle, hiding behind foliage. Yes, Terry was the man-eater in the bushes, waiting for the prey to come close, then - he would strike!

His coffee arrived. As he stirred it, he scrolled down Liv's page, checking for recent comments.

They were evil. It was all a front, of course. He had discovered weeks ago that each of the nutters with their wild assertions, were all actually the same person, coming from the same I.P. address. Maybe a paid internet professional.

My, my, you poor fellow. You have stooped so low!

Working quickly, starting at the top, Terry edited each post, taking out the swear words, the negativity. His strategy was to bore the attacker. If he logged on later and saw that all his abuse had been diluted, maybe he would reach exhaustion and quit. If that wasn't working, Terry had a second tactic. He used his knowledge of where the abuse was coming from to send acid in response, right up the delivery tube. The poor nerd would find his computer was rapidly filling with junk, every spare byte on his hard disk being taken up with nonsense and circular leads. Pretty soon the guy would find his computer blowing up.

Served him right. Whoever it was, they

deserved no sympathy. This was war, a digital battle, granted, but still war.

Terry saw his screen jump.

His sandwich arrived at that time, and that distracted him. But when he turned back to the laptop, he had a new challenge.

Terry had set his computer up to run many defensive programmes. He knew it was the only way to keep the international hackers at bay. He went into a deciphering programme and looked at the lines of code arriving.

There was no doubt. It was a deliberate thing. An attack.

Not to his machine, of course, which was too heavily defended for such remote programs to get through. No, someone had infiltrated Liv's computer and installed spyware. Every keystroke she made was now being recorded.

Terry put his food to one side, and tapped heavily on his keyboard for several minutes. He froze the spyware program temporarily, then set up a random number generator on his own computer, finally linking it to the portal on Liv's machine. He set the two running. It was simple: the spyware was a pot that drained off your bathwater, drip by drip. He had intercepted the pipe and sent a tidal wave back along it. The computer at the other end, anxiously waiting for news from Liv's computer, would be hit by a tsunami of information. It would take them days to disentangle it!

He picked up his sandwich again, and

chewed on it with a new sense of satisfaction. I showed them. Again.

His computer pinged.

Terry looked at the screen. He had set up a detection program, weeks ago, and it was able to follow such attacks to their point of origin and give him the I.P. address. Yes, but then a decoding program went into action, identifying the address, who it belonged to and where it was located. Even though such info is meant to be private, Well, Terry was thinking - I am a spy.

The origin was Switzerland, and it was a commercial company. A food and chemicals company.

Got them, Terry was thinking. Proof, at last. The bastards. The snivelling bastards. You'd pick on a woman, eh?

I'm taking this to Captain Gibson.

That evening, Mr Snopes took Melia out for a meal at a very expensive restaurant.

She had had her doubts from the beginning. It was a meal. It was at night. Would he consider it a 'date'?

She didn't want that. She quite liked the man and enjoyed his company, but she didn't want him to get the wrong idea. She had a boyfriend - at least, she was fairly sure she did - and she didn't want any more romance in her life.

No, the reason she had agreed to meet with this Snopes in the first place was that she hoped he would tell her more about the Snopes she knew, the young man named Greg and the person she called 'Snoopy'. So far, that had been an almost total failure. This Snopes seemed largely opaque about family relationships and the man he called his cousin was almost a closed book to him.

Secondly, Melia didn't like the way this Mr Snopes ate. He was fussy, picking at his food.

"I'd like to know where this fish came from," he said, turning it over on his plate. "You know there's a lot of mercury in fish, Melia? It depends where it comes from, of course. Japanese fishermen are particularly vulnerable. They eat tons of fish and there's a lot of pollution in the waters around the southern islands of Japan. It causes a whole basketful of diseases."

Melia supposed that Snopes would know that, being in the medical field. Come to think about it, he had been pretty vague about that too, saying he didn't like 'discussing work'. Exactly what did he do at the hospital? Why wouldn't he say?

Mr Snopes said, "At least there's less cruelty in eating fish. The animals get to swim around, live their lives, then we hoist them out of the water and ferry them back to our plate. Land animals have it far worse. If anyone saw how chickens live their lives, nobody would ever put them in their shopping trolley again."

He seemed very philosophical tonight, she was thinking. He was saying these things - not really talking to her. It was more of a monologue.

She would have liked to talk family. He was obsessed with the food industry.

"If people saw where meat comes from," he said, starting a new thread. "I mean, think about it. Suppose you ordered a steak for dinner, right here, in this restaurant, and the manager comes over and says, 'Congratulations, you've won a ticket for a trip around the slaughterhouse. You can go any day, but preferably a weekend'. Who's going to do that? Are you? Would you drive there, don the hard hat, the goggles, the gloves, the waterproof mac, and walk along the line seeing how the beasts come in, and what happens to them, every step of the way? Do you think you could stand that?"

Not me, Melia was thinking. She felt sick most days now, and the idea of witnessing slaughtering and dissecting of animals would really send her over the edge. She looked at the slices of meat on her plate. Why was he saying these things?

"Cows. Chickens. Pigs. The bases of our diet. How do they get to the shops?" he said, musing. "By the time we do our shopping, they are little slabs on plastic trays, covered in film. That's how we cope. We don't have to think about the origins."

Melia pushed the meat to one side and started on a roast potato. I prefer vegetables anyway, she was thinking.

"And vegetables," he said. "It's an illusion of choice. You looked down the supermarket aisle and see tins and packets, fresh and frozen. You think, 'What a lot of choice!' But it's the same thing, fifty seven ways of presenting potatoes!"

Ah, now that she had thought herself. Yes, tinned potatoes, frozen chips, crinkled or straight, bags of flavoured crisps. All the same ingredient. He was right about that. But all the rest - he was being really boring. A worthless dinner companion.

"And prepared food? Processed meals? Don't get me started!" he went on. "They all contain the same basic contents, with heavy emphasis on corn starch and soy beans. It's in everything! Of course, that's hard to verify, because labelling is so poor - and imprecise. You know the food companies have always campaigned ruthlessly against labelling? They don't want you to know what you're eating, what's inside of the mix. They've even said why. It might 'scare' the consumer. They said it!"

Fascinating, Melia was thinking, pushing her plate away. I wonder if I've got room for dessert, or maybe just coffee.

"Coffee?" Mr Snopes said, shaking his head. "Coffee? You know what coffee does? It scours the gut. It takes all those 'friendly' bacteria and washes them out of your system. Then you have to eat 'live' yoghurt, to put them all back in. Out and in. Out and in. It's just a never-changing cycle, going round and round. They've trapped you in an endless loop."

Melia agreed. She knew exactly how that

felt.

Right here. Right now.

CHAPTER SEVEN: Be Prepared

Liv thought she was being followed.

It had started in the canteen of the Chapman Building. She noticed a man come in and talk to a huddle of men at a table near the door. Liv's hackles rose. They kept looking over at her, staring at her. Were they discussing her?

She didn't like it. The cafe was the nicest, the most open, the best view, and had the tastiest food in the whole University, and now she felt as though she couldn't go there again. Sexism was so rife in the academic sector, she knew that, and every day she saw new evidence. Men! They were the bane of her life and her downfall. She couldn't let that happen now. Not any more.

She put her salad wrap back in the foam box it had been served in, stood up and walked out of the back door.

She deserved respect, she was thinking.

She was a poor girl from the local estates and yet, she had studied hard and worked her way up to being a Lecturer at Salford University. That was quite an achievement. Her childhood friends were impressed by that, and made her feel good about herself.

The fact she was also a millionairess, at this point, was no credit to her, of course. It was her talented brother, Stan, who had made good in the digital sector, inventing games and apps. When he died, his fortune came to her. She hadn't asked for it.

She cut across the grass outside Chapman and started towards the Media Building, where her new office was. It was when she was passing the Library that she felt she was being followed. The hairs on the back of her neck were rising.

There were so many people about, going this way and that, it didn't seem possible to notice. But most of these young people had little purpose. Maybe they had lectures to go to, but the majority seemed happy to stand, mill about, talk, gossip and waste time. Liv, of course, was heading for a destination, and the fact that somebody might be on the same path, it stood out.

She had a scheme for such an eventuality. She ducked around the Engineering Building and opened the back door to the Library. Not many people knew about that entrance, since it was designated 'Emergency Exit' and looked as though it couldn't be opened from the outside. But she knew the combination for the keypad. She keyed it in and dodged inside.

'Library'? It was more like a giant Games Hall now, she was thinking. There seemed to be less and less books and more and more computer screens, every time she stepped across the threshold. It didn't impress her. She could see that a lot of the so-called 'researchers' were checking their mail and social media accounts. Wasting time! It made her tut in irritation.

Liv came out of the main door, looked around and was relieved to see no one looking her way. She had given them the slip.

She walked back along the broadwalk, under the trees and through the massive arch to the new Media Building. She opened the door to the West Staircase and walked up to the third floor. That's my exercise for the day, she was thinking.

There was a young man standing outside her door. He was holding a ring binder. Student or staff?

"Olivia?" he asked tentatively.

She shook her head. No. Everyone called her 'Liv' but it wasn't a contraction of Olivia. Her given name was worse than that.

"I'm researching autism," he said.

Liv stopped, deflated. She took a huge breath. She would have asked him, 'Have you been following me?'. but that seemed irrelevant now. He had surprised her, with what he said. She hadn't been prepared for that.

"Come in," she said lightly, and put her key in the lock.

She made him a cup of tea - it seemed only polite - let him take one of the easy chairs by the door and settle himself.

He said: "My Departmental Supervisor told me you were interested in autism. He thought you might want to hear about what's come up. It's ground-breaking stuff, new figures. They're pretty devastating, I'm afraid."

Liv nodded. She sat down opposite him, let him talk. He was a young man, younger than her. Perhaps fresh from school to University, then straight into research. He hadn't taken the detours in life that had slowed down her progress.

"Tell me," she said, wondering whether it would be important to her and her obsessions.

"It's chemicals in the environment," he declared, his words definite and defiant. He sipped his tea.

Liv took another breath. Secretly, she had been convinced it was all due to inheritance. Her idea, whether or not you developed autism as a child was due to the genes that you inherited. That was what took her to see her granddad, a visit that had taken such a disastrous turn. The day after she had found her Gran battered and bruised, the old lady had died in the hospital. Her granddad had been taken into a Nursing Home and was now confused and silent, being looked after for his own good.

The police were investigating.

The prospect that the poor man ended up there, like that, was haunting her dreams and making her sad. The fact that such genes might be circulating in her family and might have led to her younger relative developing autism, now seemed very likely.

But not anymore.

That was great! she was thinking. It's not our fault! She wanted to heave a huge sigh of relief. She wanted to cheer.

Then she saw something that puzzled her. The young man was getting more papers out of the computer bag he was carrying. As he rummaged she saw the words on the front. It said, 'Chemical Convention 2015'. Underneath it said: Dubai. Under that, there were some letters, and they seemed familiar, very familiar. It didn't seem right, anymore. It seemed off.

It said: 'S.I.'

That same day, Dolf had to go into Regional Office and explain to the boss how they nearly lost Mr Marks.

He knew what Gibson would say. Where was Mickey? Well, he wasn't there. Where was he? He didn't know. Maybe gallivanting with his girlfriend, Melia, Dolf might be thinking - but he wouldn't say.

The fact was that neither of the senior agents were on hand, and it was left to the Juniors to cope, which they didn't.

Why were they in Manchester anyway, the Captain might ask, in his usual, irritated way.

As it happened, Gibson was in a surprisingly flat mood. He didn't say anything, just let Dolf tell the story.

Dolf sat down in the hard chair in front of Gibson's desk. He felt uncomfortable from the start.

"It was Mr Marks's idea," he said, trying not to make it sound as if he was blaming the visitor.

Their guest said he wanted to see the place

where Dr Jenner was shot. That seemed an odd request, but it was early morning, (the day before they were talking now), and nobody had yet had any breakfast. It seemed to be a good idea to visit a cafe. They could all dine while they were exploring. Besides, it would take them out of the Safe House, and they all needed some fresh air.

Still, Dolf insisted they do a check before they left.

Right, who have we got? Dolf, Wilkins and Sillence, on the staff team. Their guest, Mr Marks.

That would leave the Safe House empty. Dolf didn't like that idea, so he phoned Control, and they said they would send a pair of operatives along to go in and keep an eye on the place. Good. Dolf didn't want to get back and find that some bad guys had broken into the house and laid a trap for them. He hated ambushes. He wanted some welcoming faces for them when they returned.

Now, equipment. The agents all had mobile phones and weapons. Dolf watched while they checked their pistols. Working and loaded. Good. He looked at each of them. They were all wearing casual clothes, more or less modern. They wouldn't stand out in a cosmopolitan city like Manchester. That was important. They didn't want to be obvious.

Mr Marks was wearing a suit. He looked the typical dapper businessman. Dolf had been told that the cafe in question was just off Deansgate,

more or less the city centre. There would be
dozens of 'Mr Marks' walking up and down there.

They were planning on taking the tram.
Again. Parking in Manchester was a nightmare,
they all knew that, and they felt freer, more
flexible. But then, as they were discussing their
route, it started to rain. Mr Marks looked
unimpressed. It does that a lot here, he observed.
The residents of the area scorned such criticism,
but they couldn't deny the facts.

Dolf drove, backing the company car out of
the drive, and going sedately out of the suburban
tree-lined streets and onto one of the arterial
roads that led to the city. The rain continued, and
it led to congestion, of course. They crawled
along, enjoying the sights, while time passed and
their hungry tummies groaned at having to wait
for food.

As it happened, Wilkins knew that there was
a multi-storey car park near to their destination.
Back of the shops, he said. Turn left here, now
right. They found themselves in a narrow, one-
way road, but sure enough, there was an
entrance.

Dolf stopped the car. He didn't like the idea
of taking his honoured guest up four floors, only
to have to walk him down again. Too many dark
corners in car parks, he was thinking. Not a good
plan.

"Sillence, you park the car and join us when
you can," he ordered.

The girl looked less than pleased to be given

the servant's job, but she hid her feelings of oppression, and obliged.

The men stood back and let the car mount the ramp, then turned, backed up along the road and turned the corner. It was a mere few shops along the street and there was the seedy cafe called 'Miles', just as Mickey had told them it would be.

"Where is your wife today?" Mr Marks asked Dolf.

The secret agent was baffled. Why would he want to know?

I saw you checking your phone earlier. he said.

Dolf felt embarrassed. Yes, well, while he had been staying at the Safe House, looking after the Swiss businessman, his bride had been forced to make her own amusement, back at the flat. They needed to keep in touch. They were newly-weds.

"She said she's going shopping this morning," Dolf told the man, anxious not to share personal information.

Mr Marks waved away such considerations. Ask her to join us, he said cheerfully. Dolf sent a text.

The three men went into the cafe and found a seat. There was a menu on the table, but there were also blackboards on the walls, listing 'Specials' and bargains. Marks looked around, soaking up the atmosphere. I want to know how Mickey felt, he said, meeting the good Doctor here. It must have been quite unsettling, he said.

He insisted they eat first, whatever else happened. So they thought about it, ordered and waited. Sillence arrived, then did the same. Tea and coffee was brought to the table, and the food would be following shortly, they were assured.

"I don't need to know your selection," Captain Gibson said snappily. "Get on with it."

Right, Dolf replied. Okay, I'll get to the point.

It was after, after we had finished eating, and chatting, and looking. After all that, Well, that was all Marks had said he really wanted to do. Look.

"So, we had a plan," Dolf said. They would send Sillence for the car, Dolf would pay and they'd wait in the doorway.

"Where was Kiko?"

Dolf stared. Gibson wanted to know? Well - No, he had to think about it. Oh yes, she was reading a newspaper she had found on a side table. She was bored: she didn't understand Marks's conversation, so tuned out. She read, politely.

"She wanted to carry on shopping," Dolf recalled. So they left her there, to do her own thing.

Wilkins was at the front, practically on the pavement, and Dolf and Marks were lurking in the shadow of the doorway.

Then Wilkins shouted: "Shadow!" and pushed them back inside.

It was a prepared Code Word. It meant danger was approaching. He had seen something. He dived forward, ducking behind the nearest car. There were cars parked all along the narrow street. What was he hiding from?

A moment later a motorbike came level with the cafe, slowed, practically stopped. The pillion passenger was holding something up. It was a handgun. He was waving it at the cafe door, but Dolf wasn't sure he could see them.

As the man hesitated, Wilkins suddenly leapt out from his hiding place, grabbed the man's wrist and thrust it up. The gun went flying. The man at the front revved his engine, as if ready to depart, but Wilkins grabbed the gunman around the shoulders, desperately trying to wrestle the man off the bike, (which was impressive, given Wilkins' recent injury, sustained at the meeting in Manchester, on a previous encounter with other bad guys).

The machine moved forward, taking Wilkins with it.

"Why didn't you fire?" Gibson demanded.

Dolf looked shamefaced. Yes, he had his gun out by then, but Wilkins was shielding the man at the back and the angle was all wrong for Dolf to be able to get a shot at the man at the front. He was completely blocked.

"Then the cab came round the corner," Dolf went on, detailing the story.

Gibson had been told about this bit, from another agent. It was the most important thing, he was thinking.

The Black Cab, the taxi, came hesitantly around the corner, right in front of the motorbike. The bike driver swerved, to go round it, and the cab changed direction, moved forward and slammed straight into the bike, tossing the riders off and onto the road.

A civic-minded citizen coming to the aid of the forces of law and order, one might have thought, but it wasn't that simple.

Bartoli was in the cab.

Bartoli, Mr Marks's chief personal assistant, was sitting in the back but saw what was happening. It was he that instructed the cab driver to get lethal and aim for the motorbike trying to get away. He was ruthless. It worked.

Then Sillence came around the corner. She saw the bike driver getting to his feet and trying to run. She couldn't possibly have known what was going on, but seeing a fleeing man in a crash helmet, instinct took over. She drove straight for him and knocked him off his feet. She leapt from the car and placed him under arrest, with the aid of handcuffs.

Meanwhile Wilkins had the other man on the ground and was trussing him up too.

It was a good clean operation. The only sour note was when Mr Bartoli came out of the back door of the cab with a gun in his hand. He looked mean, as if he wouldn't be satisfied until he had shot a few people. He had to be dissuaded.

"He has a permit for that?" Dolf said, truly

baffled.

Gibson nodded. Marks had some sort of Diplomatic Status, which entitled his bodyguards to be armed.

"There are a few issues we are looking to discuss with Herr Bartoli," Gibson said flatly.

Dolf paused. He had relayed the stark facts of what happened. The missing parts of the jigsaw were: One, who were these assassins. Two, who sent them. And Three, how did they know where Marks was, at that precise time?

As far as Dolf could see, there was only one possible answer to that last one.

There was a spy in the camp.

That was the issue that he really wanted to raise with Captain Gibson. He wanted the boss to reassure him that the Unit would be looking into it. Which one of the team was a traitor?

Because there was one thing that Dolf knew for certain.

In this case, when it came to these particular circumstances - it wasn't him.

Talking of Bartoli, on that day, Melia was in the hospital because of him.

She had been summoned by Mickey's friend Don, a detective sergeant in Manchester C.I.D. He phoned her and asked her to meet him in the main foyer of the hospital. He wouldn't say anymore. She didn't know what it was about.

Don was waiting when she walked in the main door. He turned and greeted her with a warm smile.

Melia liked Don. She always had. In some ways he was her friend as much as Mickey's. In some ways, she thought he was a lot like Mickey, but a kind of mirror image. He was blonde while Mickey was dark. But he was just as tall, as broad. As handsome.

"You're being very mysterious," she admonished him.

He tried to smile, but he was being serious.

"If I'd told you, I didn't think you would have come," he said. "Look, Melia, it's always a pleasure to see you, but this is business." He turned and waved down the corridor. "You remember the last time you were here, recently? You were sitting in the Waiting Area at the end there, and two men came over and sat down beside you."

Melia shivered. Yes, she did recall. It wasn't fun, and if it hadn't been for Terry -

"Terry made a complaint, so we reviewed the CCTV," Don told her. "We got a clear image, blew it up. Put it out."

So? Melia couldn't think what the problem was. It would be pretty far-fetched to think that Don would have caught them.

"They turned up," he said.

He led Melia down the main corridor, but then went through a side door and they were outside again. They followed the building around and came to a small, squat self-contained block to the side of the recent development. It was entirely separate.

A sign over the door read: 'Mortuary' in large black letters.

Melia hesitated at the door. Don took her elbow and supported her for a moment, while she breathed deeply.

It was as bad as she feared. Don took her through several doors and they arrived in a corridor with a glass wall.

"Here?" she asked dumbly. Those men - they were here?

"If you're not up for this - " he said kindly, but she shook her head. No. Of course she could cope.

Don tapped on an intercom, said a few words and blinds were pulled back.

There were two bodies lying on tables. A person in a white coat and face mask pulled back the sheets covering the faces.

Melia gasped. She wasn't horrified, or shocked. She was more astonished about the unlikely coincidence.

Yes, it was the two men who had surrounded her that day. How had they come to arrive here? What was going on?

"What happened?" she asked Don.

"They were shot by a man called Bartoli. We're already looking at him for what happened at the meeting you went to the other night. You heard the shooting? Two men were killed. That was surprising enough, but now this."

"My life was in danger," a smart voice said,

moving into the area.

It was Mr Marks. He had arrived. From where, she didn't know. For why, she didn't know.

"I employ a gentleman called Bartoli," Marks said to Melia, as if trying to explain. "His job is to protect me. When we were at the Ken Wilber lecture the other evening, you were confronted by two attackers. Your friend Mr Snopes incapacitated them, but they later escaped. These are those men here. They found me in Manchester today, while I was out conducting business, but Mr Bartoli managed to surprise them and take their guns away. When they continued to resist, he had to defend himself."

Melia was confused. These were the men from the hospital? And from the lecture? Then what were they doing those two times, targeting her? And why did they move on to Marks? Had they given up on her?

As far as she could remember, these men didn't do or say anything that could be seen as a threat to Mr Marks. The other night, the evening lecture, that was another pair of thugs who arrived later, and they got shot by Bartoli. Yes, she got that.

Marks said: "The one thing we know about these two, for sure, is that they have nothing to do with Crapanza."

That was an odd thing to say, Melia was thinking. Who did have 'anything to do' with

Crapanza? The other two?

Nobody had suggested any such thing, had they?

Marks added: "Sergeant Fellowes, I have seen these bodies and I can identify them as the people who appeared in front of this young lady at the lecture. You can add my name to the list of people who have identified them. I shall now leave."

"Thanks," Don said, trying to sound as if he meant it. "We will be in touch," he said, about the other two.

"Who are they, Don?" Melia whispered as Marks walked out of earshot.

"That's the problem, we're not really sure. The one on the left had a Mexican passport with an obviously false name. The man on the right is called Tom Leamington, according to his paperwork."

Melia shook her head. No, that didn't sound right. She had heard that name. Mickey had mentioned it, hadn't he?

"Yes, well, it is odd," Don agreed. "A man by that name worked with the man Mickey met, Dr Jenner. But that Tom Leamington drove off a cliff last week. At least, we found a body in a burnt out car and the car was definitely registered to Tom. If that wasn't him, then how did the real Tom get from being a biologist to becoming a hired killer, and get himself shot by Mr Bartoli?"

Melia had no idea. She had nothing to offer. Also, she felt awkward and scared. She wanted to go.

As she turned, Terry came hurrying into the building. He was clutching a file of papers. He looked preoccupied.

He nodded at Don, then focussed on Melia. He had been looking for her, he said.

"Liv sent me over some research from the University of Salford. It's important stuff. It affects your baby," he told her.

Don was puzzled. He knew Terry, but only a little. He knew he was a bit of a nerd, working with Mickey and Melia.

"Why are you worried?" he asked, genuinely concerned. Why should Terry get involved in that sort of personal business?

Terry turned to him. "I thought you might have heard," he said quietly. "I'm convinced by now that it's my baby."

Later that day, Captain Gibson packed his gumboots and went to visit his old friend, Farmer MacLawn.

When the Captain knew Tony MacLawn, of course, he had been an agent, not an agriculturalist. It was for that reason that the boss of WSB was willing to take time out of his busy schedule and travel out of town. He supported his staff, past and present.

As Gibson's car came to the end of the long lane that led up to the farm, he was astonished to see a line of police cars along the road. There were men in uniform milling around, cops, and they were putting blue tape across the road.

The Captain parked and got out. A policeman came wandering over, but Gibson showed his I.D. and the man backed off.

"Sorry, sir," the young man said. "I didn't realise it was that serious."

It was serious enough to generate a huge police presence, Gibson observed, whatever 'it' was. But No, the police wouldn't have expected British Security to turn out, obviously. They wouldn't have known about any connection.

Gibson walked along the lines of police and came to the scene of the action. There was a tractor on one side of the road, in the field. There was no hedge or fence here, so it had obviously just come off the tarmac and driven onto the freshly ploughed earth. It was on the other side of the road from the MacLawn farm. Tony stood on that side, looking angry.

There was a police inspector talking to him, trying to calm him down.

Gibson strolled up, trying to look benign, and introduced himself. "What seems to be the problem?" he asked easily.

The Inspector stared at him. If you don't know what 'the problem' is, sir, he seemed to be saying, then what the hell are you doing here? Still, he was too old, too polite and too deferential to say any such thing out loud.

"Maybe the farmer could explain himself?" the Inspector suggested.

MacLawn was happy to oblige. He looked

forward to talking to somebody who might actually listen to what he was saying.

"They plan to plant up their field with G.M. crops," he told Gibson, "which is bad enough. But this afternoon they brought that tractor onto site. They're wanting to spray their land with Crapanza's latest and most lethal herbicide first."

Gibson nodded. That would be problematical for Tony?

"I run a certified operation," he said, irritation creeping into his voice. "I don't use any of their chemicals. Nothing as inorganic and long-lasting, at all. But if they spray there, yards from my boundary, and a single drop of their killer spray blows over and onto my land, then I stand to lose my certification. All of it. My living then collapses, but of course, they know that. It's deliberate."

"Come, come," the police inspector said quickly. "They are proceeding in a completely legal manner."

It may be legal, Gibson was thinking. But it's unethical, selfish, uncaring and cavalier.

We can't have that.

Gibson stepped up. He was smart, ramrod straight, but not tall. The police inspector towered over him. He wasn't fazed.

"I'm taking over jurisdiction," he informed the cop. "I am ordering you to stand down and withdraw your men."

The Inspector stared, lost for words. Then he paused, seemed about to say something, took a breath. Paused again.

A police sergeant, in uniform, was standing at the Inspector's elbow. He was waiting, expectantly.

"Sergeant," the Inspector said to him, "tell the men we are going back to Longsight. Get everyone out of here."

The sergeant's mouth flopped open like a fish. He was surprised. He thought the Inspector was made of sterner stuff.

But the Inspector knew the realities. If this was declared an area relevant to British Security, he had no status anymore.

MacLawn was staggered to see all the police people obediently climb into their cars, one by one, two by two, turn their cars in the narrow road and make off, out of the area. It was growing dark, and they put their lights on to see their way up the lane.

"Thanks, Boss," Tony said to Gibson. He felt as if the old man had saved the day.

"It's not over yet," the Captain observed, seeing a man emerge from behind the tractor and approach them.

The man was square, squat and swarthy. He appeared Mediterranean. He had sallow skin and hair that looked as though it was combed with olive oil. He was not a man who made a lot of friends, from the look of him.

"May I enquire what exactly is happening here?" he enquired, looking surly.

Gibson introduced himself, and said: "I have

taken command of this operation. Whom am I talking to?"

"My name is Bartoli. I report directly to Mr Marks, a gentleman you know well and are happy to protect."

Gibson smiled. It is our pleasure, he agreed. Still, Marks wasn't there, was he?

"My advice to you," he said directly to Bartoli, "is to move that tractor before it gets damaged."

Bartoli looked over his shoulder. "Oh, I don't think that will happen," he said, self-assuredly.

"Oh, I think it will," Gibson said confidently, and, stepping around the man, proceeded towards the machine.

He knew it was a gamble. If he stepped off the road and onto the field opposite, then he was trespassing, technically. It would count against him in any future investigation. So he kept his distance. He was a good three metres from the tractor.

Without looking round, he said: "Gun," and held out his hand behind him.

MacLawn placed a pistol in his palm. Gibson smiled. He knew he could always rely on Tony.

Taking aim, the Captain shot out the rear tyres of the tractor. The rubber was shredded and hung loose. He waited.

There was no noise from behind him. Maybe Bartoli was too shocked to know what to do next.

So Gibson raised the gun again and shot the

front nearside tyre. It exploded, with a satisfactory sound.

The boss of WSB turned. The gun was still in his hand, raised. It pointed directly at Bartoli's chest.

Go on, it seemed to be saying. Do something. Be a hero.

Slowly, methodically, Mr Marks's key hatchet man was weighing up the odds.

"You have a gun," he observed. "But there is only one of you."

"Two."

Gibson knew something that his adversary did not. Tony MacLawn was no fool; he would only hand over his gun if he had a spare. And today, being not only angry but also well prepared, he had two guns in his pockets.

The second was now levelled at Mr Bartoli's back.

Front and back. To an observer, it would seem that the little greasy man was completely surrounded.

When the reality of his situation dawned on him, and he realised he was a victim, he came to a conclusion.

"I have better things to do," he snapped.

With wary looks over his shoulder, he moved away, up the track. Gibson and MacLawn were surprised to see that he had a motorbike parked further up the lane, under a tree. They watched, guns in hands, while he put on a crash helmet, started the bike, then proceeded slowly past them, down the lane towards the road. They didn't relax until he had disappeared from view.

"One day," Gibson mused, "we are going to have to deal with that man. I may need your help."

"Say the word, Boss," the farmer said calmly, "and I'll get him a ticket out of here."

The Captain handed the pistol back to its owner, looked at his handiwork with pride, and smiled a rare smile.

"Now," he said, "I think I have time for a cup of tea."

"My wife bakes a wonderful fruit cake," he was told. "If you've time, you could come in the house."

"For you, Tony, I always have time."

The two men walked up the road and turned off at the path to the farmhouse. Old friends, enjoying more time together.

The two most dangerous men in Salford.

CHAPTER EIGHT: Trapped, in more ways than one

It was early morning, and Liv had been called to report to the Vice-Chancellor's office at her University.

She didn't realise that academics got up so early. They didn't. The person sitting in the Vice-Chancellor's chair was some kind of lowly minion in Administration. They worked in External Relations, they said.

Ah yes, Liv replied, when introduced. I have an 'external relation' too, she's called Melia.

"You're not taking this very seriously, Ms Livingstone," the young man said.

"Livingstone is my first name, not my surname."

The man consulted his notes. He took out a pen and made a mark on his papers. It was in green ink.

"We've had complaints," he said.

He read some out. They were short sentences, mostly abusive. They strayed into the realm of the profane.

"That's not correspondence, is it?" she commented. "They're 'comments', aren't they? From Faceplate."

He nodded. Well spotted. Yes, that was right. The negative comments were from her account, mostly.

"My personal account," she informed him. "Right, so you're calling me here, today, to tell me off because some trolls have seen fit to waste their time calling me all the names under the sun. What is the point of that?"

"It reflects badly on the University," he told her, as if it was obvious.

Liv chewed her lip, thinking about it. Maybe it was because it was so early. She had been forced to drag herself out of bed, barely had time for her usual porridge before having to call a taxi to get her down to the campus on time to make the appointment.

She said: "Let me start again. I'm getting rude stuff on my page - which is my own private page, not the University's page, or even the Departmental page, to which I contribute - and you're saying it makes YOU look bad?"

"Us," he corrected her. "It makes us look bad. The University. Most people know who you work for, I think we can assume that."

Liv paused again, waiting to see if there was any more, but the man's head was down, as he kept reading.

She asked: "What effect would this have on you? On us? On my colleagues, my Section, my research?"

"Exactly," he said. "It could have a profound effect on your research, if the funders saw this."

Liv took a deep breath, as if she was finally feeling her age. She stared at the man. He was more of a kid, really. He looked like a teenager.

What was the University doing, giving positions of responsibility to kids? Who had employed him?

"You need to check your facts," she told him, speaking slowly and clearly. "My research is funded by The Stanley Foundation. You may have heard of it. It's a great supporter of Salford University. It even has its own plaque in Senate House."

"Exactly," he said. "You've made my point precisely. That is what I am getting at. They might be upset."

"They are me," she told him.

She had set up the Foundation with money that her brother Stan had left her when he died. She named the Trust in his honour. It gave several bursaries to students and supported several lines of research, including her own.

Liv said: "In a sense, I am self-funded. You might say, I am self-supporting."

He stared at her, temporarily lost for words. He looked at her through his glasses, as if they were microscopes, but he couldn't see through her. He could see nothing. He couldn't read her. He had no idea if she was making it up.

Liv added: "I think we should leave it there."

She stood up, pushed her chair to one side untidily, uncaring, didn't bother looking at him as she left the room.

He said nothing, not having anything to say. He looked at the clock over the door.

It was looking like a very bad start to his

day.

Outside, on the broadwalk, Liv, still seething, turned her feet towards the Chapman Building, thinking about coffee.

She didn't notice the man lurking in the shadows of the Library, not until he stepped out and accosted her.

"You don't know who I am, do you?" he asked wearily.

She stopped, momentarily flustered. It was the young researcher, from the other day. The one who talked about autism.

"My name is Jeremy Jenner," he said falteringly.

Liv stood stock still, rooted to the spot. Then she felt tears erupting from her eyes, and she stepped forward and brought the youngster into her arms, sweeping him up. They cried on each other's shoulders, for quite some time.

Luckily, she had tissues. She wiped her eyes, then his, then they walked together towards the student canteen.

"I'm doing this research for my father," he told her, when they were settled down with steaming mugs of coffee. "He inspired me, yes, but he also gave me direction. He gave me the names of chemicals, I looked into them, and yes, he was right to be concerned. There were two things they all had in common. One, they all have serious side effects."

"What was the other thing?" Liv asked,

interested.

"They are all manufactured by Crapanza."

Liv looked at her coffee, trying to make sense of it all. One company. Could it be causing so many problems, worldwide?

He said: "There's only one thing that worries me. They must know. They have their own research teams, dozens of people, in labs and manufacturing plants, in many different countries. They test, all the time. The results I'm finding, they are out there, in the records. So how can the company go on making stuff that they know - they know for sure - are causing problems?"

Liv nodded at that. But that wasn't the thing she was thinking about, that wasn't the 'one thing' that worried her.

It was the simple fact that this man had once had a father, and now he didn't, possibly because of something Dr Jenner had found out, or said, or maybe raised as a concern.

Perhaps he had put it on Faceplate! Yes, when Liv put stuff on social media, she got told off.

The Doctor had been killed, maybe for the same offence.

That wasn't just worrying. It was unfair. Unjust. It was totally over the top.

But Dr Jenner had a son, and here he was, doing similar things, looking at the same information. Asking the same questions.

How long before the company decided to

have a go at silencing him?

At that moment Terry was knocking on the door of Captain Gibson's room in the Regional Centre.

It was early, the boss was looking at his diary, working out what he was doing that day and the rest of the week. He was cross-referencing with notes he had made, and emails he had received. So many invitations! The Northern Powerhouse was finally getting a head of steam. It could take over his entire calendar, he was thinking.

Terry put a report on the table, a Matter of Interest, that he had received from the London office.

"Summarise," Gibson said snippily, not wanting to have to read another page.

Terry obliged. "A food researcher at Swansea University has been shot dead on campus," he said.

The Captain nodded. That was bad. That was unusual. How many people were murdered at Universities? Not many. A few.

"His name is Dr Jenkins," Terry added, and let that sink in.

Gibson's eyes widened. You don't mean - he seemed to be saying.

Terry nodded. "It could be a case of mistaken identity," he suggested. He was clearly rattled. Not happy at all.

Gibson put aside his papers, clearing his

desk. This matter deserves my attention, he agreed. Terry was right.

Terry was clutching a sheaf of paper, individual pages that he had glued together into one big chart.

"I have made a Family Tree for Dr Jenner, the man that Mickey saw gunned down," he told the boss, and spread it out.

That seems a long time ago, Gibson was thinking. A lot has happened since then.

A lot had. Terry pointed to the name at the top of the page, Dr Jenner, and followed the lines up, down and sideways. Children, siblings, ancestors. The names in black are surviving, he said. Those in red are recently deceased.

The map was a mass of red ink.

"Murdered?" Gibson gasped, incredulous.

No, Terry couldn't say that. But all dying within the last six months, either through violence or accident, misadventure or carelessness. Those furthest back were the most mysterious, having all suffered unexpected and untimely ends.

"This isn't just killing," Terry suggested firmly. "This is genocide."

Somebody, the Captain saw, from the evidence, is doing their damnedest to wipe out the entire family.

A name sprang to mind.

"Crapanza," Gibson intoned huskily.

"Let me tell you something about Crapanza," Terry said.

It was all over social media, he started. It was new.

The company had been sending researchers to faraway places for many years, looking for new compounds, new medicines, new cures. It's like aspirin, he said. Sure, we have been using that in the West for many years, but when the gang arrived in South America, they found a little-known tribe, deep in the jungle, who were used to chewing the bark of a local tree when they had sore heads. The company men took some samples and managed to isolate the active ingredient.

"Their version of aspirin," Gibson suggested, but Terry shook his head.

"No, it was aspirin," he said.

But since it came from tree bark, Crapanza could patent it as a new discovery, or, at least, protect the extraction method and get themselves a new corner of the market, sell the product and boost their profits.

"But it's aspirin," the Captain protested.

No, it's 'tree-derived painkiller', Terry said. It's a 'new' compound in the world, as far as the legalities are concerned.

"That's baffling," Gibson said, shaking his head.

About as strange as Crapanza trying to patent the common carrot, Terry was thinking, but he didn't want to stray there.

"Meanwhile, back in the jungle," he said, "the team found a sweet root that the same tribe had been putting in their drinks for years. It's a completely natural sweetener, and the natives called it 'Bilbombo', or something similar."

So that's another addition to the Crapanza product list? Gibson asked.

Terry nodded.

But there's two scandals that come out of this story. Two.

"One," he said, "is that the company has found a way to process the root and sell a purely chemical compound. They've renamed it 'Sweeterest' and they'll be manufacturing it by the ton and selling it to the drinks industry."

"Good for them."

But not good for the natives. The researchers took away the info, made their own version and secured a patent. Which means that Crapanza is going to make millions out of their 'new invention'. The people in the jungle will get nothing.

"You said two problems," Gibson prompted.

The other problem is a bit closer to home. It means that Crapanza are launching this new sweetener now - it's one reason why Mr Marks is in the country, to organise that jamboree - but it gives his company a stranglehold. They will now have two major sweeteners, if you count 'Sucrosanct', which Dr Jenner came up with, all on his own.

Terry said: "It's insurance for Crapanza. They want to get free of the Jenner connection, and they've tried to achieve that by offering to buy the family's interest out. If they can't achieve that, they can simply stop making Sucrosanct and start making Sweeterest. Either way, they won't have to shell out money to the Jenners. The Jenners' future income is denied."

If that wasn't bad enough - Well, the thing that occurred to Terry, mulling it all over, is that Sweeterest might not even exist. Knowing the company as he did now, it seemed entirely believable. Why not keep on making Sucrosanct but pretend that it's a different product, a new thing called Sweeterest? Easy. Cheat the Jenners without having to find anything new in any jungle!

Gibson sent Terry back to his box. He accepted all the papers, and said he would read them thoroughly.

But when the door was shut, he turned his chair around and faced the wall. He suddenly felt very old.

It's the way business is done today, he was thinking. It was never like this when I was young.

The bad stuff - the stealing of people's inheritances, whether the tribes in the jungle or the tribe called Jenner - and the completely ruthless way that patent law was now exploited to profit big business rather than reward people who earned the right to really benefit, it was new, it was different. It was a product of a new political philosophy, a 'dog eat dog' outlook that they seemed to be teaching in modern Business Schools and in the Head Offices of the major companies.

It had never been like that in his day. Business people had principles then, integrity. They could be justifiably proud of what they achieved. This lot - they were like a new wave of Robber Barons, valuing self-aggrandisement over everything.

It was a misreading of economic theory. In the past, business was aware it was part of the community, and took pride in protecting and rewarding their workforce. Now, only the shareholders derived rewards. Everyone else got screwed.

It was also a misreading of Darwin's evolutionary theory. He had written that life progressed through the 'survival of the fittest', but he meant 'fit', as in the fit of a piece of a jigsaw, the way a species fitted in to their local environment. He didn't mean the Tarzan approach, with the fittest being the one with the biggest muscles and the toughest killer instinct. It was fanciful, a fantasy.

Most of all, it was childish. Big business was now being run by kids.

You could tell that because they didn't acknowledge any of the duties that adults face.

If you grow up, maybe you'll marry and have kids. Those children have to be protected, nurtured, educated. Sometimes the little darlings get sniffles and have to be cared for at home.

Sometimes they get ill and have to be rushed to hospital. Sometimes they get in trouble and parents have to go to school and talk to the Principal. Sometimes the kids get picked for the School Play, or the football team, or get an award for bravery. The parents need to turn up.

They can't. Their employers expect them to be in the office early and leave late. They have to put in long hours, and they can't have even the shortest amount of time off for 'personal reasons'. That would distract them from their primary duty, to make money for the company.

But adults, true grown-ups, can't be single-minded. They have duties and responsibilities, to family, spouses, even their neighbours. They have ageing parents of their own, and siblings. Even friends to keep contact with.

But modern business says No. It says 'leave all your other concerns at the door, and give me 110% while you're in the office'. That's how stupid big business has become, Gibson was thinking. There is no such thing as '110%'. It doesn't exist.

The perfect employee doesn't exist either. Unless you can find a young man with no romantic attachments, no family, no outside interests, no imagination, and no emotions at all. In other words, the perfect worker would be a 21-year old male.

No wonder then, that the Board Rooms and offices of banks, insurance companies, manufacturers, and real estate companies, are stuffed full of fat, over-fed, middle-aged men acting like teenagers, with the outlook of 21 year-olds.

No responsibilities. No worries, no cares, no interests - except the well-being and growth of the employer.

Kids, wedded to a false philosophy and a vacant ideology, which had never worked in the past, and was not working now.

They had harnessed platitudes and falsehoods from Darwin, distortions which fitted the wisdom level of juveniles, and it explained the obsessions: continuing expansion, never-ending growth, climbing every mountain and fording every stream.

Why else was it that the energy companies couldn't stop drilling? Ever. Couldn't turn away from what they knew. Look for other resources, other methods? Things that might actually survive through the coming century.

The total denial that oil and gas would ever run out, or that fossil fuels could ever lead to problems in the atmosphere?

Gibson stood up and shook himself. He looked in the small mirror on his bookshelf. I'm getting old, he was thinking.

I respect Business, he knew, but it had to be responsible, mature, caring, aware of the good and the bad it could do.

It has to be Mature, he decided. Otherwise we are all lost.

His job, for forty years, had been to preserve

the country in which he was lucky enough to be born.

His nightmare, right now, was that the old enemies - out East - were a mere sideshow, and that the real threat, the people who could bring Western Civilisation to its knees, were out there in tower blocks in the city, making decisions that materially affected the well-being of millions. And what did they do? Sip champagne and congratulate themselves on their blinkers.

They needed to look in a mirror, he was thinking, as I am doing now.

They need to see who they are, what they're doing, and what they're risking.

Otherwise, it will be 2008 all over again.

And again. And again.

Melia was in court that day.

It wasn't for her. It wasn't even for one of her friends, directly. But MacLawn had phoned and told her what was happening. He asked her, if she could spare the time, to go along and see how things might turn out, and report back.

Melia agreed. Anything for Tony. She liked the man. He was one of the few people she could rely on.

Besides, it occupied her thinking, as well as her activity. That was good. She didn't want to think right now. There was far too much to think about. There was her future - or the lack of it. There was her support - or the lack of it.

Mickey? It seemed like he was doing the

same thing - working so hard, such hours, that he had no time for her, or talking.

If she stopped to think, she would have been sad. Better to avoid that, she concluded.

The tractors got in the way.

They were all across the road outside the Crown Court, blocking traffic, causing a stir. It brought the newspapers down, and the other media. It was an event. From somewhere, close by, Melia could hear a jazz band playing. It was a carnival.

There were hundreds of people milling around, some with placards. All looked extremely angry.

That was the first point then, the first item to put in her report for Tony. Whatever this thing that was being heard today, there was a crowd of people who felt involved, who seemed to think it might mean something to them. They wanted to make their point.

It was about Crapanza trying to steal a local farmer's crop, and his land. It wasn't MacLawn.

No, not MacLawn, but the thing that MacLawn had predicted, it was happening.

A lawyer, a Crap lawyer, was standing in front of a camera, explaining to the TV News that his company was 'totally justified' in pursuing a claim in court, since 'tests proved' that their crop had been found in a neighbouring farmer's field.

That was theft, the man asserted, and that was the story he would be putting to the jury in the courtroom.

The 'truth', as predicted by Melia's friend Tony, was that the wind had blown blossom from a Crapanza strewn area into a free and independent farmer's territory, right next door. It was their carelessness that had caused the 'problem', not his.

Only he wasn't there. The farmer. The 'defendant'. He hadn't appeared this day, despite being summonsed.

His daughter was there to explain why.

He had committed suicide.

Melia got closer, so she could hear the girl's story. It was heart-wrenching. He had become depressed, convinced that the legal letters from the Crapanza company had sealed his fate. He would lose the farm, he told his children, and it made him feel awful.

He couldn't bear the guilt. He disappeared. The police found his body in the River Irwell a week later.

His daughter wouldn't cry. She told the tale, and she would repeat it in court, later. She didn't plan on shedding a tear, not until everyone had heard, the company had been condemned for its heartlessness, and she had won her case.

That would be difficult. She had no representation.

It had been an unproductive harvest, she said. She had no money for legal help. She couldn't afford a lawyer.

She would put her own case. Eloquently, no doubt. But Crapanza had a legal team, Melia could see. Four of them.

"She doesn't stand a chance," an educated voice whispered in Melia's ear.

She turned. You know about these things? she asked him directly.

He smiled. He was a tall man, thin, very well dressed. He carried a briefcase. His hair was fashionably long, and floppy.

"Why don't you represent her?" Melia demanded.

The man smiled, an educated smile. "I would love to, my dear, but I cannot afford charity, sadly."

Melia looked over his shoulder, and a thought formed in her mind.

"If I was to guarantee your fee," she said slowly, "would you take the case?"

"Have I your bond?" he asked, extending a thin and delicate hand.

I'll pawn the farm, Melia was thinking, as she gave him a handshake he would never forget.

He looked around. "As soon as she finishes with the hyenas of the Press, I will take her to one side," he promised.

Melia watched him slide away, slippery as an eel.

Then she turned the other way, and marched through the crowd. She had spotted someone she knew.

It was Liv.

She had Terry on her arm, and she was moving this way and that, as if looking for someone.

That would be me, Melia decided.

She strode straight across to her, grabbed her shoulder and spun her cousin around. She had no time for pleasantries.

"Brought your cheque book?" she asked.

In a few short sentences, Melia explained the situation to Liv and she nodded, less than enthusiastically, but an agreement was good enough, Melia decided. She hugged Liv. You won't regret it, she assured her.

"Pay the man," Liv ordered Terry.

Terry had his small computer with him. He could make a funds transfer from here, he agreed and went off to find the lawyer.

"Stan would be proud of you," Melia said to her cousin, tears in her eyes. Spending his money wisely, after all.

"I should hope so," Liv said. I honour his memory, she said, which is why I'm looking for you.

I have a proposal for you, Liv added. A suggestion. I've talked it over with Terry, and he agrees.

"We will look after your baby," Liv said. "Give it to us. You know we can give it a safe, secure and loving home."

Melia was speechless. She wanted what - it made no sense! Melia would be a good enough mother.

"You have a career," Liv reminded her, "with little time off, and constant danger. It's not fair on the kid."

Melia felt her stomach turn, like somebody was stirring her insides. She felt physically sick.

How could Liv think of such a thing? How could she cook up such a fantastical plot? Melia blamed Terry!

Melia put a hand to her mouth. She felt like retching. Her head was spinning.

"Oh, God, Melia! God," Liv said, looking down. She reached out, afraid and desolate.

What? Melia was thinking, her vision going, darkness descending.

"Melia, you're bleeding," Liv wailed. "Help! Somebody, help!"

The person who might have helped, might have been in the best position to help, was Mickey. But he was several miles away.

Mickey was at the Water Treatment plant. He had been called back, by the same keen young man he had met earlier.

"It worked," he told Mickey. "It worked. It worked!"

He was practically hopping up and down on one foot. Bent over the CCTV monitors, he looked ridiculous.

At the last visit, after Mickey had almost fallen off the top of the main stack, Mickey had talked - briefly - to the kid and suggested some 'improvements' they could make to their security on site. He never thought the lad would do it.

The young man was toggling the display,

enjoying showing Mickey how clever he was.

"You were right," he told the older man. "You said they'd come back, and they did. Only this time, we got them!"

He showed Mickey footage of shadowy figures coming around the boiler building and moving along the walkways. It was exactly what must have happened before, when unknown individuals had broken in and sabotaged various pieces of equipment, such as the ladders, gates and grab handles on the stairs. Not satisfied with their first efforts, they were obviously trying again.

"Okay," the youngster said. "Okay. We did what you said and paired the cameras, so that as they walk through we get front and back shots. That means we know they're the same person, each time, and we have 360 degrees of body. We also have two chances at their faces. Even though they're wearing scarves, I've managed to meld the shots in the computer, and Bingo! Nearly a whole face. Your tech guys should be able to get Facial Recognition to work on what we can give them."

Brilliant, Mickey agreed. That's some evidence, at least.

That's just the start, he was told.

The base team had also re-arranged the entrance, so that any intruders would have to go through a series of doors to get into the offices of JenCo. That would be their destination, they all knew that. So, working on a predicted route, the kid was able to set up what was, in effect, an air lock. The burglars would be between two doors and all the air in between could be isolated.

It was based on a theory that most of the dust in a house or office was nothing more than flakes of human skin.

What the bad guys wouldn't know is that the area of the 'air lock' was having its air supply scrubbed at regular intervals, depending on usage of the corridor. When the burglars came through, they would trigger the pumps and the filters.

"We've got their DNA!" the kid enthused.

There was no way the baddies could guess they were being surveilled or sampled. But the air would have been cleared in front of them, and then, after they had passed along. Which meant, any tiny fragments of skin left behind, had to be theirs.

Getting a clear DNA print from such a small sample was hit and miss, but the kid worked for Termack. They had the kit and the engineering. He was able to run the test a couple of times, and he got lucky. Both men gave clear profiles.

The youngster handed over small bottles and print-outs.

"I've no idea how you're going to compare these to police records," he said, but then, he didn't want to know.

He had gathered the data, and that was his enthusiasm, his work, and his life. He felt he had done enough.

"That other thing," Mickey said, prompting. He wasn't sure if the kid had gone all the way, but the youngster answered with a grin.

"We get a mix of guys on the gates," he told Mickey. "Some of them are foreign workers, reliable but not adventurous. You were lucky. Padric was on that night. He was one of the few I managed to convince, and he kept the tracker by him in the shed."

It was simple. The intruders had parked their vehicle up the lane, making the rest of their way into the site on foot. But when they clambered over the fence, it triggered the silent alarm. Padric, at his post, at the entrance, was able to see them entering. Then all he had to do was switch on the infra-red cameras along the road and look for the vehicle with the warm bonnet. If the cars belonged to workers on the Night Shift, then the engines would be cold, since they'd been on duty for hours. The hot car belonged to the recently-arrived burglars. Simple. So all Padric had to do was skulk along the pavement and place the tracker in the wheel arch.

"Ta da!" the youngster said, switching on another monitor. It showed a map of Manchester. A red dot was bleeping.

"That's the car?" Mickey asked, in wonder.

"That's the one," the kid told him. He had been watching it all day. It was driving all over the area, but still local.

We've got them, Mickey was thinking. Evidence. Solid evidence.

"So who is it?" the young man asked. Engineering companies, trying to copy new and innovative technology? Energy companies, trying to find ways to defuse new and sustainable ways of producing electricity?

Mickey didn't think so. It would be biology or pharmaceutical companies, wanting to find the mix of bugs and 'friendly bacteria' that were being used in the Digester. After all, they could patent that cocktail and make money selling it on.

"Someone like Sagar?" the kid suggested.

Mickey nodded. Yeah, maybe.

But much more likely was a more famous name. The one that belonged to the headlines and the gutter press. The one that already had an established reputation for stealing, spying, bribing, threatening and intimidating.

A name like Crapanza.

The company that the egregious Mr Marks worked for and currently represented, while he was in the country.

Mickey was going to enjoy going to see the man.

He couldn't wait to hear his excuses.

CHAPTER NINE: Nasty threats

Terry had organised himself breakfast with some criminals.

He wasn't feeling proud of it, which was why he hadn't mentioned it to anybody. Specifically, Mickey or Melia. He knew what they would say, they would try and tell him it was 'risky'. Worse, one - or both of them - would insist on coming along.

He didn't need protection! More important, he didn't want patronising.

So, establishing excuses - he had worked late the night before - then mumbled to Captain Gibson that he would 'take some personal time' and come in around lunchtime. The boss nodded. He never argued when his staff wanted time off.

It was a lie, it was all a lie. He was meeting some people, he just didn't want anyone to know about it.

He didn't tell Liv. That was particularly difficult. He had spent the night at her house and had to get up, take a shower and pretend like he was going to work, as usual. She said something about the University, and they went their separate ways.

It wasn't a promising start to a relationship he hoped would be based on uncompromising love and trust.

Terry waved the waiter over. He hadn't yet finished his coffee, but he wanted another cup.

Ready, for when the goons arrived.

He looked around. It was 'Miles' cafe. Wow, British Security was keeping this place going, just by their patronage alone!

Still, it was a convenient place to meet, central in Manchester, yet walking distance from Regional Office. Ideal.

A pair of geeks poked their heads around the door, saw Terry and strolled over, exaggeratedly taking their time.

"Gandalf says Hi, then," the first one said, bending low to whisper.

That was some password, Terry was thinking. Still, it established their bona fides.

"Sit," he told the two, and ordered them coffee. They seemed agreeable to that - if Terry paid.

They were younger than he expected, Terry was thinking. They looked more like school kids than anything, but that didn't make them innocent. They were in danger of ruining his life and he had no sympathy for them.

Terry reached under the table and brought his laptop computer out of his bag. He opened it on the table top.

"This is the infected machine?" the second one said. He was the one without glasses. And black hair, dyed.

You should know, Terry said. You infected it.

Terry said: "Let's just discuss how this goes. I give you money and you unlock my keyboard.

That's about it?"

"We didn't have to do this in person," the first one said, but he was a bad actor. He couldn't keep a smile off his face.

He was completely pleased with his own cleverness.

Terry told him: "Oh, but I wanted to meet you guys. It's a clever program. Very effective. It's completely screwed my machine."

The kids looked at each other, nodding, happy. Yes, it does that, they seemed to be saying.

And yes, we send you the virus, it plays merry hell with your computer and you have to come to us to fix the problem. We dictate the terms. You pay us what we want, and you get your photos, music, emails back.

It's embarrassing, Terry was thinking. Back in Regional Office, the whole network was protected by layers of firewalls that he had designed personally. But one night, round at Liv's house, he had taken out his laptop, logged on to her wifi, and got himself scuppered in seconds. When the blackmail screen came up, it was more of a relief than anything.

At least he knew it was human interference, not an unsolvable bug in his system.

Humans could be dealt with, he knew. (If Mickey had been there, he might have punched them, of course. That was his method.)

Terry brought out a brown paper bag and laid it on the table-top. He let the youngsters have a glimpse of the rolls of ten pound notes inside. There were hundreds of them, it seemed. It was a tempting view.

"Let's get on with it," Terry suggested. He needed to get to work, after all.

The first young man pulled a laptop out of his back pack, and opened it on the table, screen touching Terry's.

"Fire yours up," the kid said. "There's wifi in here, right? Yeah, there is. I can see it."

Okay, it was simple. They had sent a virus to Terry's machine and locked it. Now, using the café's broadband connection, they could simply send the antidote across to Terry and unlock the gate. He would be back in business in seconds.

The kids were smiling again, at each other, stealing glances. This was obviously a lucrative business, Terry was thinking.

"Should be anytime now," the second kid said, his hand hovering over the bag of money.

Terry tapped his keys. He seemed irritated. He looked baffled.

"Nothing," he said. "You sure you know what you're doing, you two?"

The one with glasses was offended. "You sure you do?" he snapped back.

Terry spun his computer round so they could see the screen. It was a mass of squiggles, just as it had been before.

The first one gave a frown. That shouldn't be happening, he was thinking. (He could see the money drifting away.)

"Let me see yours," Terry said angrily, spun their laptop to face him, and tapped a few words on the keyboard.

It all happened so fast, the youngsters had no time to realise they had been suckered.

Not until their screen started dropping letters, like rain, from the top to the bottom. There were howls of protest.

"What did you do?" the pair wailed.

I've just proved I know a lot more than you do, Terry said. You've met your match, kids. Admit it.

What he had actually done was link their computer to a website that he had set up from the office. He typed in the address when he grabbed their machine, and it started downloading mess and garbage immediately.

Two can play at this game, Terry was thinking proudly.

He stood up, folding his machine. He could take it in to the Regional Centre now. It was unfrozen and he could install plenty enough protective measures before these 'amateurs' would be able to retaliate.

He started to walk away, revelling in the consternation he was leaving behind. The mouse catches the cat, he was thinking.

The second one said: "What about the money?"

Keep it, Terry laughed. Why not? When they started to count it, they would be disappointed to find the cash money was only the top layer of each bundle. The rest was newspaper, cut to size. Another con! I'm the King of them, Terry was thinking.

As he walked down the road, back to the other side of the river and his comfort zone, Terry had one or more other thoughts.

Mickey would have handled them, he knew, but in the way that Mickey did things - with his fists. It would have worked, of course, it was always an effective approach. But that's how wars started. Terry, on the other hand, had played them at their own game. They were nerds? Sure. Knew computers? Maybe. But not as much as Terry did. He was an expert, a professional.

He had made a slip, Terry knew, but then he faced his failure, acknowledged it, and worked around it. Then he came back with an even more effective counter-measure. He could have done it online, of course, but he was curious: he really did want to know what these pirates looked like. Well, in real life, they were pussy cats.

He had taken them.

But he could. He knew that, and knew something else, something far worse. That if he hadn't been who he was, then at some point - maybe when his laptop first seized up and he flew into a murderous rage - he could cheerfully have killed those guys. If they'd appeared at the Office, and someone had put a gun into his hand, sure, he would have fired. He was that wound up.

But that was anger. That was the pure red rage you can sometimes get in the heat of the moment.

What happened to Jenner - and what was continuing to happen to his family - wasn't anything like that.

It was sheer, cold-blooded, cold-hearted murder. Crimes of passion were understandable. Murders of Jenners were not.

Whoever was doing it, whoever had instigated the campaign, whoever was running it now, was not human. They were some kind of a reptile of a human being, with ice water in their veins and not a shred of compassion in their hearts.

God, Terry was thinking, I hope Mickey finds out who it is pretty soon, and I hope he uses all his ruthlessness.

Shoot the bastards, Mickey, he would be shouting! They deserve it.

No forgiveness! No mercy!

But Terry had another secret, something else he couldn't share. He had deciphered Dr Jenner's USB pen.

It had some stuff inside. Wow, it was explosive! Terry realised. It could bust the food producers wide open.

But there was a problem.

Most of the documents were Jenner's own reports, his findings, his Memos and correspondence. In other words, there was no corroboration. If the material came to light, the companies would simply say: "Interesting allegations. Prove it!"

There was no proof on the memory stick.

There should have been. Maybe Memos from the company. Maybe Minutes of meetings, or chemical studies, medical research. Anything that had their logo on the top, or their Executives' names at the bottom.

It was like someone coming up to you and saying, 'Hey, have you heard this? It's wrong, all wrong.'

Terry had no doubt it was, but he was truly confused about how to lay out the stuff. It wouldn't stand up in court.

After puzzling it over for a few days, Terry came up with a plan. It wasn't much of a plan, but it was all he had.

Firstly, he would say to people that he had nothing. He would deny that the USB was readable.

That would throw people off the scent, and make them look elsewhere for the source of rumours or innuendo.

Because, second, there was going to be plenty of that.

Terry was going to take the 'allegations' and drip feed them one by one to bloggers, commentators, News sites and social media. He would introduce the claims as interesting ideas, ask for comments, start a discussion.

Most important of all, he wouldn't use his name on anything - but set up a stack of aliases - and not mention the Jenner family either, any of them. That way there was no one to blame. But, and this was the clever part, the companies would know that they had been rumbled. The things they were trying to hide would all be out there, in the public domain.

They would never feel safe again, knowing they hadn't managed to plug all the leaks and stifle debate.

It would keep them awake at night, at least, and keep them on their toes when they were planning the next outrage.

For more direct action, Terry was still relying on Mickey coming up with something.

Something a bit more tangible.

Terry didn't know it, but Mickey was actually on the case at that very moment.

He had returned to the old Jenner home, with Dolf, to have another look around. He was convinced they must have missed something, but despite an hour and more looking under floorboards and at the back of cupboards, there was nothing.

Then it had to be the Treasure Map! Mickey reasoned.

Obviously, Dr Jenner didn't trust anyone, not even his own family. His wife had told Mickey that her husband 'brought work home', but clearly he brought it and took it back. He didn't leave anything behind. Maybe he reasoned that if the company thought he did, it would give them an excuse to raid his house. He didn't want that. He had striven to leave the family out of it.

It hadn't worked, of course. Mainly, because he had no idea how downright savage his opposition was.

He had underestimated them.

There was a knock on the door. Mickey wasn't worried. He knew the place was up for sale; it would be the Estate Agent, showing a hopeful buyer around the place, maybe. That was a good thing. The sooner the house was bought, the sooner the family would get the money. It would help them. They were under pressure.

Mickey was right. It was a young girl with a clipboard, leading an old man in a suit, the buyer. He smiled at them both and welcomed her.

"My boss warned me you gentlemen might be working here," she said.

Mickey smiled. "We've finished up in here. You can have the place to yourself," he said, then seeing the visitor looking concerned, he added: "Simple survey. Don't worry, we've found nothing untoward. The place is in good condition, considering its age." He laid it on a little, but then, he didn't want to be the reason a buyer might be put off.

Mickey led Dolf out into the garden and shut the doors firmly behind them.

"Follow me," he muttered. "We have some digging to do."

He led the way across the grass to the shed by the hedge, opened the bolts and looked inside for tools. Mickey selected a spade, passed another to Dolf, and took a garden fork too. They might need all the equipment, he thought.

With spade over shoulder and map in hand, Mickey led the way along the canal bank.

Dr Jenner had obviously tried to highlight landmarks, but the results were unclear. A rectangle on the water could have been a boat, or maybe a mooring. A square on the other side could be a house, or maybe a garden. Still, Mickey could see that a circle in the lower left hand corner had 'No 79' written on it, which was Jenner's house number. Working away from that, and the fact that a wavy line across the top of the page had to be the canal, Mickey deduced that the round things were trees. Counting along, the 'X' that marked the spot was about a hundred yards from the start, with other crosses behind it.

There was a hedge. Mickey looked over the top and saw, not another house, but a church. With a graveyard!

That had to be it, he concluded.

"Okay, team," he told them. "Start digging!"

Between them, taking it in turns, they managed to make quite a hole. Luckily this wasn't the side of the canal that had the towpath on, so they wouldn't be blocking anyone's way. It was late autumn, Mickey was thinking, when it wasn't his turn to dig, and it was cold. Only the person doing the work was getting a sweat. They might be there all day!

He was wondering if he could go back and ask the Estate Agent to make them a cup of tea, or whether that was sexist, when there was a clunk. Dolf was in the hole. He looked up, pleased with himself. Then, just to prove it wasn't imagination, he tapped the ground again and there was the ring of metal on metal.

The spade was hitting a metal box.

Between the two of them, they got it free and hauled it onto level ground. Dolf smashed the lock open with his spade.

He whistled. "I don't think I've ever seen solid gold bars before," he noted.

Mickey reached in. There were a few of them. Quite a few. Also, down the side, there was a small silver key.

"I think those must belong to me," a voice said.

They all turned. It was Mr Marks, and he wasn't alone.

Dolf's Thai bride was standing right beside him.

Mickey was shocked. Dolf looked less than surprised, but maybe a little disappointed.

Dolf said: "So, you know him. We've all been thinking there was a traitor in the team, and everyone thought it was me. Of course they did. I don't have a very good track record. But that time in the Cafe, we were going out of the door and a motorbike arrived, with a gunman on board. We left you in there on your own. You got on the phone and called them. You let me down."

Kiko looked a little confused, not sure, maybe, what he was saying. Her English wasn't that good.

Marks was looking from one to another. He seemed irritated, more than anything, as if wanting them to sort it out.

"Look, people," he snapped, "I don't care who does what, just put your muscles into it and get my box of Crapanza gold back to our car. We can sort out the details later."

Mickey picked up a gold bar, idly, as if inspecting it. At the same time, he managed to palm then pocket the small key.

"No identifying marks, Mr Marks," he commented. "Aren't these things meant to be labelled with source, grade, date and so on? If they aren't, then they must be contraband, stolen maybe. Illegal certainly. You sure you want to claim them?"

Marks took a step forward. "Don't play me around," he said. "You know Jenner couldn't possibly - "

A shot rang out.

Mickey turned to one side, in alarm. Dolf had a gun in his hand and it was pointing forward.

Marks was looking around, as if he expected to be shot. But he wasn't. Nothing had happened to him.

Beside him, Kiko was sinking to the ground, holding her side. She let out a small sigh, then fell flat.

"She had a gun in her hand," Dolf claimed, looking mean. "It was her or me. I had to do it."

Mickey took a deep breath.

This is going to take some explaining, he was thinking.

Back in Manchester, Melia was on her way to the hospital again.

She wasn't ill.

For once in her life, she didn't feel that bad. The regular sickness was wearing off, and the scare she'd had the other day - with the bleeding - was inspected, considered, assessed, and declared to be not so worrying. She'd rested, then been dismissed.

No, her mission that afternoon was to see Mr Snopes.

Not that he was expecting her. In fact, he was under the impression they would meet that evening, but Melia had been thinking about the man quite a bit, and come to the firm conclusion that she didn't like him. She was going to see him now - before the night's date - so that she could confront him and tell him the bad news. She didn't want to have to spend another boring date, eating food she didn't like and listening to views and opinions she found it even more difficult to stomach. She needed to break it off, she decided, whatever 'it' was. For that was the other problem. She was convinced that this particular Snopes was seeing their meetings as more than just friendship. She hated to disillusion him, but it was true. She had no feelings for him.

It had taken her a while to realise. At first,

she had been thrilled to be in his company. But it wasn't him, she came to see, it was the man he represented. Greg Snopes, the man the other one alleged was a 'cousin', was twice the man this one was. He was special. He was a true friend, and it was a real honour to have known him and spend time in his company. This new Snopes wasn't anywhere near his league. He wasn't even in the same ball park. He didn't match up. Sorry.

Melia had wondered if there was any way to break such news gently, then concluded that there wasn't. She would have to be straight, be brutal. She would have to tell him: Thanks for the time, but I think we need to stop seeing each other.

She wondered, a little, what he might say? Maybe he would think it was Mickey that was coming between them. Melia chuckled to herself. If only it was that simple! If they were 'love rivals' then, sure, Mickey would have won. But so far he hadn't revealed himself as anywhere near the domain of 'love' at all. Melia was still waiting for him to get back to her.

Pretty soon, it would be reaching the point of no return. She had a baby growing inside her. Did he even care?

Melia knew where Snopes worked - he had told her. Down 'in the basement', he had said, or something similar.

She walked across the polished floors to the lift, and went down a level to the labs. Glass walls were on every side.

Melia walked along, humming happily, glad

she had made a decision.

She checked off the names on the doors, then saw a notice pointing around the corner to the 'Path Lab'.

Strange, his name wasn't on the door. Everyone else was listed: 'Dr This' and 'Dr That'. A cold feeling came over Melia. Maybe Mr Snopes wasn't the man he pretended to be. Maybe he wasn't even a Doctor. A lab assistant, merely?

Then she saw another sign and was stopped in her tracks. It read 'Crapanza Wing'.

In a hospital? The chemical company had sponsored their own research department? They had that much money?

She paused in front of a glass window. It showed a number of workers in white coats bent over laboratory equipment and benches. Even from the back, she recognised one of them as Snopes. He was moving Petri dishes and taking notes.

In front of him, directly in front, was an open ring binder with several printed sheets of paper visible.

They were headed: 'Crapanza: Statistical Data'.

Melia turned, then leant up against the glass, feeling light-headed again. She found herself fighting for breath.

It wasn't just that this man had made himself out to be someone he wasn't. That was shocking enough. It was also that the company she had only recently become acquainted with was turning out to be a real octopus, with arms in every pie, every building, every organisation she was having any contact with. Had they infiltrated everywhere?

Mr Snopes, she kept thinking. I'm so disappointed in you.

But more than that: she didn't just want to prise him out of her life anymore.

She wanted to kill him.

Later that night, Mickey was relaxing at home.

He'd had a pretty bad day, he reflected, pouring red wine into a glass and putting on soft music.

The problem was, Kiko didn't die.

True, when the men rushed over and bent down to see how she was, she looked completely unconscious.

But then she opened one eye.

And that's when Mickey uncovered a previously hidden truth - Kiko was a karate expert.

How she managed to leap into action, practically come back to life, and bound to her feet and attack them, he wasn't sure. But in the space of mere seconds, the three men found themselves fighting for their lives.

Luckily, Marks was the closest, so he was the first to go down under a hail of blows.

Then she went for Dolf, her errant husband.

She didn't spare him. Maybe she resented the fact that he had abandoned his wedding vows and put a bullet in her. Whatever, she set about him, with all her might.

That gave Mickey the chance to assess what was happening, see her intentions and prepare for his turn. By the time she turned on him, he had picked up the second shovel, feigned a strike, turned the other way and brought it down on her head.

Marks was grateful. He said something about attending to the gold 'later' and staggered along the canal bank back to his car, to find his own way back into Manchester. Dolf and Mickey were left to clear up, with the help of back-up from Regional Office. When the other agents arrived, they were thoughtful enough to bring a van and a big wheeled trolley, which provided adequate transport for the tin box.

Mickey spent the rest of the afternoon trying to explain to his boss what was going on. Luckily, Gibson had his own concerns and didn't complain much. He was kept busy reacting to Memos from Head Office in London. They wanted his opinions on the rapidly changing situation in the U.S.A., but he had little to offer. Nobody from the Old Guard did.

Mickey stood by the window of his new flat while he drank his wine. It was dark outside, but the lights from the houses along the road were twinkling. It was nearing Christmas, so there would be coloured lights up soon, he knew.

There was a knock on the door.

Mickey's new place was on the second floor. If someone had arrived on the street, they would have had to press the Intercom button at the main door, and he would have been able to see them on hos tiny TV screen. The fact that nothing like that had happened, probably meant that the knock was from someone in the building. One of his new neighbours.

Still, some sixth sense made Mickey reach for the red button beside the door as he opened it. Just in case.

Two men in masks burst into his hallway. They were carrying pistols. They pushed him back into the lounge.

As Mickey passed the red button, he reached for it, but his hand was brushed away.

"Naughty, naughty!" a deep voice intoned patronisingly.

Mickey somehow managed to hang onto his glass. He took another sip. This was an interesting development.

"Do I know you?" he asked politely.

"No reason you shouldn't," the short, squat man said and ripped off his hood. It was Bartoli, Marks's assistant.

"You boss knows you're out late?" Mickey said sarcastically.

Bartoli said: "I'm not working on his dollar tonight. I freelance, didn't you know that? I work both sides of the street."

The tall, thin man took his mask off. Mickey

stared. I've never seen you before, he commented.

"I think you have," Bartoli assured him. "My friend here drives a motorbike."

Mickey gasped. "Then you're the guy who was driving the man who took pot-shots at Mr Marks?" he asked. Your boss?

The fat man giggled. "Marks pays, we shoot who he wants us to shoot. Someone else - well, we shoot Marks."

Confusing. Like when the man on the motorbike was driving past the cafe trying to get a shot at Marks, Bartoli was in the taxi coming down the street – In effect, on the opposite side.

Tonight, by contrast, they were working together.

A cold feeling crawled down Mickey's spine. Cold blooded killers. Then maybe -

"You shot Dr Jenner?" he suggested.

Bartoli nodded. "Strictly speaking, I'm the clean-up guy. But when I'm asked to front line, I step up."

"Then what do you want with me?"

"You've annoyed some people," Bartoli said, shrugging his shoulders, not really caring.

Mickey put down the glass. "Right, so you don't mind providing a confession, because now, or soon, you're going to add me to your list."

"That's about the size of it."

"What are you going to do about the videos?"

Bartoli looked genuinely puzzled. "You have

cameras?" Nobody had mentioned cameras. "Where are they?"

"No idea," Mickey said. "Look, I've only been in this flat a few weeks. My old house, by the park, was knocked down for regeneration and infrastructure improvement. I was practically given this, and they asked me if I wanted CCTV. I said sure, if it's in with the price, but I wasn't here when the work was done. I know all the rooms have got a camera, that's all."

"Where is the recording device?" Bartoli demanded, looking ugly.

"Oh, I know the answer to that one," Mickey said. "It's in Eccles."

The hit man started to look frustrated. He nodded his head, as if he was thinking things over.

"Okay," he said, at last. "I shoot you, I leave the country. It's about time. They won't find me where I'm going."

"If you can get out of the building," Mickey said, playing for time. "I don't think you understand the way my security system works. Before I open the door to anyone, I tap the red Panic Button. Then, when I see a friendly face, I can tap it again and there's no alert. But if I don't tap it the second time - and you stopped me doing that - the Silent Arm rings in Eccles and all the cameras come alive. There will be people looking at the monitors now, seeing all that's going on."

Bartoli was nothing if not adaptable. "Okay, I don't shoot you," he suggested. "Not tonight.

But the police might see me threatening you. That's not such a big deal. It might rate a fine, maybe. Don't you think?"

"Who said anything about police?" Mickey said quietly.

The Eccles centre is an independent security operation, he told his attackers. They are a private firm, with their own rules. Friends of mine, actually, he told them. They are more like a protection racket, actually, an old-fashioned Salford gang.

Mickey said: "The phone is going to ring, any minute now. They will want to hear from me."

Bartoli nodded. We don't have to shoot you yet, he agreed. Let's see how that goes.

The home phone rang, the land line. Mickey walked over to the sideboard and picked it up.

"Mickey? Are you all right?"

It was a local accent. Mickey half fancied he recognised the voice, but that was unlikely. Some ex-gang member?

"It's Maurice Scarrett," the voice said. "I'm not going to let them get away with it." Whatever it is.

Mickey was impressed. The boss. The Chief of the Salford gangs. He was giving Mickey the Gold Star treatment.

Well, he had said he would 'help' Mickey one day, any way he could. He said it at the cemetery, at Jenner's funeral.

Mickey asked casually: "Can you see what is

going on?"

"It's not clear. Are you free to speak?"

"That would be a negative," Mickey said, ramping up the crisis.

"Is there just the one of them with a gun?"

"No."

"Two? Both got guns?"

"Yes, that's right," Mickey said.

Mickey could hear voices in the background.

"Give me five minutes," Scarrett said.

"There might not be that opportunity."

"Make it three," the crime boss said and cut the connection.

Bartoli was looking interested.

"You've come to some arrangement?" he asked, curious to hear more.

Mickey spread his hands.

"Here's the plan," he said, laying it out for them. "They've got a patrol in the area. That's a big, black car with four guys in it. Big men with black suits on, like bouncers in a nightclub. They are equipped with shotguns. They will arrive at the front door, but two will go around to the back. You will be surrounded. Your only hope of getting out of here alive, is if I speak up for you."

"But you might be dead by then."

"You'll need me alive to keep you alive. You want to die for your boss, the one giving out the contracts?"

The thin one looked at Bartoli. He gave him a look, which said: 'I don't know who that is, do you?'

Then he said: "I think he's bluffing."

"We'll soon find out," Bartoli told his assistant, grinning. He was enjoying the tension. It was a game to him.

There was a knock on the door.

Bartoli jumped. "That's impossible. They couldn't have got here so fast."

"I told you," Mickey said. "They had people in the area."

Bartoli licked his lips. For the first time, he felt nervous.

He said to the thin man: "You still think he's bluffing? You answer the door."

The thin man looked at the gun in his hand. It seemed to give him confidence.

They all went back into the hall, the thin man stood behind the door and pulled it open.

There was no one outside.

Bartoli gestured with his gun. The other man, looking nervous, moved towards the opening and peered out.

He stuck his head out of the door, his gun held out in front of him. Then a baseball bat swung down from the left and swept the gun out of his grip, shattering his wrist. He screamed in pain and fell back into the flat, scrabbling along the floor.

Bartoli got behind the door and slammed it shut. He was breathing heavily.

His mind was racing. A bat? That didn't mean the gunmen had arrived. It could have been someone else, someone closer, who had been alerted to the danger and ordered into action by the gangsters in Eccles.

Yes, he was thinking. It could have been, say, the caretaker for the block. Maybe he was an ex-gangster, a friend of theirs.

Curiously, he was completely right.

"How are you going to handle this?" Mickey prompted, seeing the panic building in Bartoli.

The gunman looked at Mickey, then looked at the gun in his hand. He knew, in a flash, as long as he was holding that, he was the enemy. Whoever was on their way would shoot him to stop him shooting anybody else.

He strode over and then, ceremoniously, turned the handgun around and offered it to Mickey.

Mickey took it, weighed it in his grip. Nice. He checked the magazine. Fully loaded. It hadn't been a courtesy call.

Seconds later, the phone rang again. Mickey picked it up and told Scarrett he could bring his people in.

Mickey opened the door. There was the noise of pounding on the stairs and four men in dark suits burst into the flat. They were all carrying shotguns. Mickey grinned. He hadn't actually been expecting his prediction to come true, but it did.

The men searched every room, just to satisfy themselves that no one else was hiding, then stood around the hall, one in each corner, waiting for their boss to show up. He arrived, minutes later, as promised.

"Stop that man screaming," he ordered.

A thug went over and smacked the thin guy on the back of the head with the butt of his gun.

Scar surveyed the scene. He didn't like what he saw. He thought 'Home Invasion' was a dirty little, cowardly crime.

Mickey said: "Thanks. You need to thank your guy with the baseball bat, too."

Scarrett grinned. "Yeah. It's always good to have a man on the scene."

Bartoli wasn't talking. He knew he was in a bad position, but he was an important person, commissioned by many important organisations. In his world, money talked. He was thinking he could probably buy his way out, right now.

Scar was an important person in his world too, but his world was Salford. He didn't care for anyone outside the city and borough. He wasn't impressed by international conglomerates. He was the master of life and death in his fiefdom.

"What do you want me to do with this pair?" he asked Mickey. It was his choice, he decided.

Mickey was in no mood to bargain.

He said: "This man killed Dr Jenner and God knows how many of his family. He needs to disappear, permanently."

Bartoli perked up. "No," he said. "Look, I'm just the clean-up guy. I'm a professional. We can do a deal."

"Not this time," Scar said.

He was angry. His face was turning pink

with rage. My cousin, he was thinking. Jenner was my cousin.

If Mickey hadn't been there, he would have turned on the assassin straight away, pounding him into a pulp before dispatching him, with prejudice. He was 'a professional', this Mr Bartoli? Yes, but it wasn't just a 'professional' job to Scar. It was family.

He turned to his team. "Get them out of here," he ordered.

Bartoli was hustled out, protesting and complaining. The thin man was carried out, unconscious.

Scarrett came over and shook Mickey's hand.

"I guess we're even," he said.

Mickey nodded. Until the next time, he was thinking.

CHAPTER TEN: The well laid traps

Captain Gibson was apoplectic.

"I will not have a member of my team threatened!" he stormed.

He was talking about Mickey. No-one - absolutely no-one - had had the temerity to attack one of his top agents in the privacy of their own home before. This was war! He wasn't about to bow down in front of such threats.

He would take them on.

"I have indulged these people for long enough," he shouted at Terry. "Now we begin the fightback!"

He kept banging the desk, that's what was upsetting Terry. He had never seen the old man in such a temper.

He's nearly losing it, Terry was thinking. If any sane person could see this, they'd think the Captain needed locking up.

"I know you have other priorities!" Gibson was screaming down the phone. "Put them on hold. I need you here!"

He was talking to his colleagues in Leeds. Then he phoned Liverpool. Birmingham. York.

He called in reinforcements from every Regional Office in the north of England. Terry quailed. They had never had such a call to arms in the history of WSB. It was unprecedented. He wasn't even sure Gibson could do it. Did he have the authority?

The boss wasn't ordering anybody to do anything, he kept insisting, but if they ever wanted his co-operation in the future, then they were going to have to oblige now. The implication was clear; do me a favour, or else.

Gibson slammed his office phone back down in its holder, and the whole thing jumped.

"I think they knew I was serious," he said with satisfaction.

He looked at the paperwork spread out on his desk. Suddenly it didn't seem so important anymore.

He opened the large drawer in front of him and swept all the papers into it. He shut the drawer with a slam.

"Now, we are ready. Right, let me know where everyone is. Melia?"

She's at home, Terry told him. She had phoned in to say she would be in later in the day.

"Head her off," the boss said. "We don't need her here. I've no need for a planning meeting. Mickey? Dolf?"

Terry reported but it just made Gibson more irritable. Details! He didn't want little things. He was considering the big picture.

"Silence? Wilkins? Smit? Sidings? We want all our resources at MacLawn's farm," the Captain told him.

Call the team, he went on, one by one, and get them all to report to the farm.

Meanwhile, get all the backroom staff we can spare - Admin, Support, Communications, especially Communications - and re-locate them to the farmhouse. Set up a Mobile Centre there, with all the equipment they need. Get vans. Cars.

"Weapons?"

Gibson grinned. On him it looked sinister. Terry felt a chill go through him.

"All the weapons we have," the boss said. "Everything. It's no use here. I want it on site. Now."

It was not yet noon and was already looking to be a sunny day, if cold.

Down on the farm, Mr MacLawn was surveying his top field. It looked washed out, but glistened, as if there was a layer of frost across the patted down grass. It was a grazing area, he told everyone. Undistinguished. Not his best acre.

In fact, it was a body dump.

Farmer MacLawn had been planting nothing in the ground but human remains, ever since he bought the land.

The problem was that Crapanza had looked at their maps of the area and concluded that they could not make the best use of the farm they had acquired next to MacLawn's unless they gained better access. They wanted his top field to make a new road.

I can't have that, the farmer was thinking to himself. I can't have them digging up this plot.

They might find something.

They would find, if the truth be told, evidence of what he had been doing for British Security Services ever since he had officially 'retired' from their employ. In fact, of all the changes he had made to the farm, this was the one he was most proud of.

He didn't want to see it interfered with.

Accordingly, he had dug traps.

The premise was simple: if they came to inspect the field, they would probably approach from the farm track on the right, or the one in front of him. At the right, he had dug a three metre deep hole across the road and covered it with branches and bracken. Any vehicle which came up from that direction would sink abruptly into the ground. They would disappear from sight.

As for the access to the front, he had taken a simpler approach. He had planted metal crosses just below the surface. They wouldn't be a danger to tractors, but they would shred car tyres. Cars could approach, but they wouldn't get through.

It was an interesting position to be in. He remembered, many years ago, when he was an agent, reading about a householder who had been the victim of a spate of burglaries. The visitors seemed to favour climbing in the kitchen window, so the owner had taken the precaution of leaving his washing up in the sink. The next time the bad people tried to gain access, they had trodden on knifes and forks and suffered several serious injuries. What a shame! the farmer smirked to himself. They brought it on themselves.

The courts didn't agree. The householder, the man suffering the attacks, was charged with Assault and found guilty. He had to pay a hefty fine. The man with holes in his feet got sympathy from the police and was never prosecuted.

I wonder if a modern court would deliver the same verdict? MacLawn was thinking.

Well, he was willing to give it a try.

As he headed back towards his farmhouse, Farmer MacLawn was alarmed to hear the blare of horns. Cars?

He came out from behind his orchard and onto the track near his main gate. He looked up the road and saw coaches. A line of coaches. They were queuing up to get into the farm gate further down the lane. His neighbour's entrance.

Tourists? For one bizarre moment, MacLawn imagined that Crapanza was laying on coach tours.

The reality, of course, was far more worrying than that.

At first, he didn't see it. He wandered down the rutted road, taking his time, untroubled. He could see a coach edging its way into the farmyard, then noted the confusion as it tried to pull in past one that was obviously desperate to get out. There were men in front, milling around, waving their arms. They were making a pretty poor job of directing traffic.

It was crazy. It was like trying to squeeze a quart into a pint pot. The yard simply wasn't big enough. As the coach backed up, trying to get a turn and head out towards the gate, it practically tore the door off the barn.

Only it wasn't a barn anymore. Farmer MacLawn saw the rows of bunk beds. It was a dormitory.

He stormed up to the nearest man in front of the coach, a thin man in a reflective jacket. What was going on?

The man looked interested, but shrugged his shoulders. He didn't appear to understand a word of English.

Tony walked towards the farmhouse. A middle-aged lady was standing there, a large tea pot in both hands.

"I'm your neighbour," he told her. "Tony MacLawn. We haven't been introduced."

"I arrived this morning," she told him brightly. "Tea? It seems to be what they all want, even though they're not from round here."

"Where are they from?"

"Eastern Europe, mostly. They can come here now, did you know that? No paperwork. It's wonderful, isn't it?"

Not for long, MacLawn was thinking. Britain is leaving the European Community. Foreign workers are a thing of the past.

He asked: "What are they doing here? What are they going to do?"

The woman put down the pot and wiped her forehead with a tea towel. She seemed baffled by details.

"You'll have to ask my husband about that. He's Foreman Manager."

You're living in the farmhouse? Tony asked. Sure, she said, but we're not the owners.

"Who is?"

"Oh, some Swiss firm, I think. Some international conglomerate, Ted tells me. A foreign name. No idea, really."

But why would 'the firm' need such an army now, of all times? It was practically winter. What could they be doing?

"Where is your husband?" he asked politely.

She replied, but most of her words were drowned out by the roar of diesel engines as another coach pulled into the yard, crawling around the outside of the last one, which was still in the process of backing out. The door of the new one popped open, and bodies piled out. Dozens of them.

Tony got the gist. He followed the woman's outstretched arm, around the side of the barn and into what should have been the far field. Only it wasn't. It was a street. The farmer stared in wonder. A series of shacks and sheds had been constructed, leading off into the distance. There were habitations, shops, coffee places and cafes. They had been hastily constructed, then. Almost overnight.

He had seen something like it before, on

television. It was like the refugee camp in Calais, built by immigrants.

A man in a donkey jacket came stomping along, pounding his feet on the duck boards, kicking up mud and water. He spotted MacLawn and seemed to know him, even if Tony had never seen this person before. He reached out a hand to shake.

"Like it?" he blathered. "It reminds them of home. All the comforts they had across the Channel, before they got here."

Was it even legal? Tony stared, at the man, at the line of shanty buildings. Then he saw something in the distance.

His blood ran cold. It was a pair of white men in suits, the duplicates of the ones who'd come to visit him before, threatening him with legal action. The gentlemen who had so mysteriously disappeared. Here were their replacements.

To do the same job, presumably, harass him, force him to comply. Ruin his farm, his livelihood, and his life.

Oh my God, MacLawn was thinking. Am I going to have to fight them all?

He needn't have worried. Captain Gibson had arrived, and he was determined to help and assist his ex-employee.

It had been hell to get in. Gibson's convoy had been blocked by coaches, a dozen of them in the lane, but he had sent his agents out to remonstrate with the drivers, and the larger vehicles had been forced to pull over and make space to allow the cars to get through. There was muttering, grumbling, but the Captain had the law on his side. He wasn't afraid to use it.

His team pulled into MacLawn's farmyard but were surprised to find there was no sign of the farmer. Where had he gone?

Form up, the boss ordered. I want Section Heads to report to me, here, for a planning meeting. Then we deploy.

The smooth operation was somewhat disrupted when scouts came back with information that there was a line of young men forming on the side of the lane that divided Tony's farm from the one opposite, the one where the coaches were going into.

Were they doing anything? Causing trouble? Not at all. But a line of men was worrying. What could they possibly do? There were all sorts of potential actions.

Gibson ordered all his NCO's to get their squads into a defensive position along the boundary of MacLawn's farm. That put them down the near side of the road. Facing them, not three metres away, was a line of young men, one every metre.

There were hundreds of them.

I want answers, Captain Gibson was thinking. What were they doing there? What use could that Crapanza farm possibly make of so many dozens of fit, healthy and energetic youngsters. The only time he had seen anything like it was when farms around where he grew up hired contract pickers for the fruit harvest. Then, dozens of young people arrived. But, firstly, that was in summer and autumn, not early winter. And second, there were girls too, and older people as well.

Here, there was no spread of age or gender. The young men looked all the same, tough, and speaking no English.

A helicopter buzzed overhead. That's not mine, Gibson was thinking. Then he heard the squeal of sirens.

In short order, a dozen police cars came crawling up the lane, then drove sedately between the ranks of men facing each other, and into MacLawn's yard. They parked, and began unloading. Police in uniform. Bobbies. Cops. English cops.

One of them was an Inspector, the same Inspector that Gibson had faced before, and treated meanly.

"I hope I'm not intruding," he said politely, walking up, inspecting the situation coolly.

"We didn't send for you," the Captain pointed out.

"Nobody did," the Inspector agreed, smiling warmly, "but my job is to uphold the law, and that is what I am here to do."

On what side? Gibson asked cynically, so far, unimpressed.

The Inspector took him to one side. "Last

time," he admitted, "I was a bit confused. But I'm British, by God, and I'll be damned before some Goldilocks investors come in here and disrupt my way of life and my country. I hope I can assure you of that."

Gibson smiled, impressed despite himself.

"We could probably use your help," he had to agree.

"I see your line," the Inspector said, turning back to the confrontation. "My men are rather good at that, standing in line, preventing encroachments on land that does not belong to corrupt businessmen and people who throw their weight about."

A deal was done. The police would take up the defensive position, while Gibson's men could deploy somewhere more useful, in the likely eventuality that another threat developed. Gibson was grateful for that, but did the Inspector have enough troops?

"We are the forward detachment," the policeman said with confidence. "Now I am here, I can call for our main force."

In the next hour, a succession of minibuses delivered police in uniform into the staging area. The Inspector took great delight in arranging them in lines, with groups to back them up, at intervals.

Meanwhile, Gibson moved his Communications staff into the farmhouse and set up a Base. He was instantly in touch with the other operatives coming in from Yorkshire and

Lancashire. He began to plan his strategy.

"I've got drones up in the air," Terry told him. "You really need to look at these pictures."

Terry had live video of the barns at the back of the farmhouse, and the shed and shacks. It's a street, he said.

"Maybe he isn't bringing in workers for the farm," he mused. "Maybe he's simply providing some kind of Refugee Camp for all those people who were evicted from Calais." But how did he get them across the Channel? It was bemusing.

Gibson was about to say; "I don't care how they got here, I will not allow them to - " when Terry interrupted.

"There's Tony," he said, spotting the farmer at the back of his own farmhouse. What the hell was he doing?

Gibson picked up a radio and sent out a general call. Mickey came back. He was by the farmhouse.

"Go and see what our farmer is up to," Gibson snapped, "and report back."

Mickey was with Dolf. It was getting to be a regular pairing. In some ways he was almost becoming used to it.

You're not as attractive as my usual partner, he kept saying. Dolf wasn't offended. In fact, he agreed.

Mickey relayed their orders. They circled the farmhouse and came to a small orchard. They walked through the fruit trees and came to a hedge. There was a picturesque wooden gate. Dolf got to it first and reached to open it.

"Stand back!" the farmer warned, seeing them trying to come through.

Wise words. Just beyond the gate was one of his traps, and he had caught a big one.

Mickey stepped forward, then stopped, stunned. It was an unbelievable sight.

A large black car, possibly German, had fallen front first into an enormous hole, a trap which straddled the lane. There was no way to get past the vehicle, or, from the look of it, to back it out. Even the boot of the car was below ground level.

Mickey looked at MacLawn, who was standing five metres away, past the lip of the indentation. He was smiling broadly, pleased with his guile. Mickey shook his head. He had always respected the guy, this ex-operative, but now he seemed crazy.

There was a crashing from below as a man in the front of the car tried to get his door open. There was no room on the driver's side, so he scooted across the seats and opened the passenger door. There was little space to operate, but he got the door open enough for him to squeeze out. Then he hauled on the back door of the car on that side.

A face looked out. It was Mr Marks.

"What the devil are you people playing at?" he snarled in tortured English.

Mickey sighed. Isn't this the man our Unit is

tasked to try to protect? We seem to have led him into harm's way.

"You're trespassing!" MacLawn yelled at him. He was unapologetic. What are you doing on this land? he demanded.

That was a fair point, Mickey was thinking. This lane was at the back of the property. You wouldn't need to come down this way to visit the farmhouse. They were behind that building. Whatever Marks was doing, it was suspicious.

Dolf leaned over and offered a hand. I can probably get you out, he suggested.

With the chauffeur below, and Dolf above, they hauled Mr Marks onto level ground. I want to speak to your boss, the industrialist demanded.

That suited Gibson. When Mickey came in, leading the disgruntled businessman, he was positively pleased to see him.

"I'll accept your explanation," he said to Mr Marks, "although I probably won't believe a word of it."

Mr Marks declined to be interrogated. He seemed to have developed a huge sense of his own importance overnight.

"I don't have to explain myself to anyone in this country," he stated firmly. "My responsibilities lie in Switzerland."

Gibson looked at him. He seemed to be weighing him up. After a few moments, he decided he should take action.

"My demands are that you evacuate the farm opposite and withdraw all the new arrivals. You can send them back to wherever they came from, or build them a Reception Camp in your precious Switzerland, I don't care."

"Your 'demands' - "

"My second requirement is that you immediately and forever desist from all attempts to harass Mr MacLawn. He is under our protection and we will use the full force of what we have available to defend his life and property."

"That man - " Marks spluttered. "That man has just about nearly killed me, with his stupid hole in the ground - "

Gibson wasn't listening. He indicated to Mickey and Dolf that they should bring Mr Marks with them, and they all went out to the back of the Base and into the farmyard, where it was quiet. Gibson turned to face the foreigner.

"I need you to know I'm serious," he said with vigour, and told his men to take one each of Mr Marks's arms.

The Very Important Person was now stretched out, his suit hanging off him, still creased and muddy from the trap.

The Captain took off his jacket, hung it on a hook by the back door and started to roll his sleeves up.

Mickey was shocked. Gibson never took off his jacket! He had never seen it before.

The boss of WSB was a good foot shorter than his guest, but he didn't hesitate. He walked up, ducked low and smacked a fist into the Swiss businessman's midriff. The breath went out of his victim in a rush. He was gasping.

Mickey and Dolf were holding him up. If they hadn't, he would have collapsed.

"You can't - " he muttered, gasping for air. "You can't do this."

Gibson hit him again, fast and low. He practically buried his fist in the man's overblown gut. It sank in fat.

Marks was flabbergasted, lost for words.

The Captain paused, considering his work. It was a useful start, he was thinking. I'm not finished yet. I can continue.

"Wait," the victim said, as Gibson approached again. "Wait! All right, I get the point. You've convinced me."

"Why don't I believe you?" Gibson said conversationally, and hit him again, as hard as he could manage.

The visitor was doubling over in pain. He opened his mouth and his lips were flapping, but he couldn't speak.

"You think you have connections," Gibson told him. "You think you are valued in this country. Not by me. Not by us."

Marks nodded, pained and embarrassed. His brain wasn't working. He couldn't plan his revenge.

Gibson walked up to him and, bending down, put his face next to Marks's.

"You think you can fight the whole of the British Army?" he demanded.

Mr Marks shook his head. No. That really was beyond him. He had met his match. He knew he was beaten.

The Captain waved to Mickey and Dolf, and, as one, they let go. He flopped to the ground.

"Mickey!" Gibson said, retrieving his jacket and walking back in through the door. Mickey followed.

Dolf bent over the gasping man. He was waiting for him to recover. Then, he might offer him a hand up.

"Sorry," he whispered. "Sorry. I hate for this to happen to you. But I had to keep up my cover. I couldn't reveal myself."

Marks stared up at the agent through moist eyes.

This man still works for me? he was thinking. I can't remember.

Meanwhile, back at the front line, Melia had arrived.

She had found a lift as far as the main road, then walked the rest of the way, past the coaches, dutifully lined up, and then the police cars, and, finally the Unit vehicles. Blimey, the whole gang's here, she was thinking.

The walk did her good. She had been feeling a little off, but the weather was bright and sunny, if a little cold. She had dressed well and was feeling cheerful. She was looking forward to the future. She was beginning to think she could cope.

She found herself in the middle of the stand-off, police on her right and young men on her left. Who were they? She heard the youngsters talking to each other, muttering under their breath. She didn't recognise the words. East European, maybe?

Melia reached the farmhouse and saw the agents milling. She recognised a couple of guys from the Leeds office. They were talking to each other, furtively, but when she came closer, they turned and smiled.

"How's it going?" she asked, returning their smiles.

One developed a frown on his face. "Dave says he recognises the language," he said. "He worked in Africa."

Africa? Melia asked. She thought they looked European.

People from Estonia and the Baltic settled in South Africa, Dave explained. It was never a large community, and was always under pressure, being ignored by both the Dutch-heritage settlers and the black indigenous population.

Melia nodded. Fair enough. So what are they saying? she enquired.

They were standing at what was effectively the end of the line. Dave suggested they approach the youngsters nearest to them. They could do it without being noticed, maybe. The police wouldn't like it, it would look like 'fraternisation', not the kind of tough-guy image the police were trying to promote. But Melia agreed with Dave and his mate. Yes, let's be discreet, she told them.

The trio moved along the line till they came to the end of the young people, which fortunately was almost out of sight, as the track curved around the end of the farmhouse. The police line only went as far as the WSB operatives standing outside the farm, so there were no police close enough to see them. They were almost hidden, out of view.

The guy called Dave drifted up to the last man on the line, acting casual, smiling, bobbing, trying to look unthreatening. He got chatting. The 'East European' didn't look unfriendly, Melia noted. The visitors seemed happy to chat.

Whatever was going on, they didn't seem to understand the nature of the growing conflict. It wasn't coming from them.

"What is he saying?" Melia said, keeping her voice low, trying to look friendly.

"He says they are Boy Soldiers."

It was like putting pieces of a jigsaw together. Each bit made no sense on its own.

Sure, these people were Refugees, and they had travelled overland from sub-Saharan Africa to the northernmost tip of France to try and get into Britain and start a new life. Yes, they had been living in a jungle camp at Calais and when the place was demolished, they were happy to accept an invitation from people who offered them jobs and somewhere to live in England. They went along with them, were loaded into coaches and driven to the port of Rotterdam in Holland. There, they were smuggled onto tankers and other, smaller ships, and taken across the North Sea to ports on the east coast of Britain.

They all notice one thing. The tankers all had the name 'Crapanza' on their flanks.

Still, the migrants had no idea where they landed or what was meant to happen. All they knew was that no one asked them for papers, and they were put on coaches again, and brought here, to the farm. They could see there were barns and shacks for them to sleep in, as well as the 'street' of cafes and shops, just like in Calais. It was home from home.

They were happy enough to stay. And work.

Melia stepped up. "What do they think they're being asked to do now?" he said to the man doing all the translating.

"They're simply being asked to stand," he said, drawing on what they'd told him.

But yes, there was no denying their history. They had been soldiers in the wars going on in East Africa. If called upon, they wouldn't be frightened to fight. Is that what the chemical company wanted? Is that why it brought them here?

The Unit man went on talking to one of the youngsters. Many minutes passed as their conversation continued.

When he turned back to Melia and his colleague, there were tears in his eyes.

"This one," he said, "has just told me some

of his story. He saw his mother and father murdered by tribesmen when he was only six. It changed his whole life. He's been living as a soldier ever since. The rebel army has been his family."

Melia sympathised, but saw immediately the danger. These young men had no families, no past. If Crapanza ordered them to line up, they would. Ordered them to shoot? They would. The company had bought themselves a private army.

"You need to get to Captain Gibson," she told her colleague. "Tell him everything. This is important stuff."

The kids in the line were looking round. They had spotted a figure coming out from behind the farm, and crossing the road to get to the other farm opposite MacLawn's. It was a flabby man in a suit that was once smart, but was now shabby.

It was Marks.

Raggedly, unprovoked, they started cheering.

Yes, it made sense. They were cheering the business leader who had brought them out of the refugee camp and across the water to the Promised Land. Of course they were grateful. Of course they saw him as a hero.

The agent who had been translating took Melia's advice, and started moving towards the Base area, to report.

The other one, transfixed by the spectacle of the cheering kids, still managed to turn to Melia and say: "What will you do?"

Melia was staring at Marks. He's the one we have to watch, she was thinking. He's the enemy, the focal point.

"I'm going to follow that slippery eel," she told her pal, and started moving to her right.

She hadn't gone more than a few metres when she saw Mickey come around the corner of the farmhouse.

She stopped, staggered at the coincidence. What was this? She hadn't seen him for days, hadn't talked to him properly in weeks. He was there, but hadn't told her? They were on the same assignment and he hadn't checked in?

"What are you doing?" she demanded, angry as hell with this on/off lover, this most unreliable of partners.

"Following the fox," he said briskly. "You wanna walk with me?"

Of course I do, she felt like muttering. I want to be with you always, you big dope.

Still, it would be better for the two of them to stick together. They had no idea what tricks Mr Marks might turn to next.

They saw him move round the end of the High Street of sheds, pass a barn and go into the back entrance of a large plastic polytunnel, the sort of farm building used for raising seedlings and weather-sensitive plants like lettuce and other salad crops.

"Shall we risk it?" Mickey asked quietly.

I'm always taking a risk with you, Mickey,

Melia was thinking. How did I ever get myself in this position - pregnant and uncertain whether the father was sticking with me or not? Why couldn't he just pause for a minute and talk to her?

They carefully opened the door to the polytunnel, quietly, so as not to alert anyone. Putting their heads in, they saw a shadowy figure disappearing out of the far door, twenty metres away. It was a huge construction, lined with shelves and raised beds. It was warmer than outside, but dim. There were a few bulbs in the roof, but the plastic skin diffused the sunlight and made it dark.

They edged gingerly along until they reached the far door. Mickey took the handle. It wouldn't turn. The door had been locked from the outside. That was strange: Marks locked it after him? Unperturbed, they went back the way they'd come, but when they got to the door they'd come in by, they suddenly realised it was locked too. They were trapped.

Neither was worried. The doors were thin wood, with plastic windows. They looked flimsy, as if they could easily be broken.

What they didn't know, but were soon about to find out, was that Mr Marks was standing at one side of the sheet plastic building, turning the taps on a bank of gas containers. They contained Crapanza's favourite herbicide. It suppressed weeds, killed them down to their roots, and wasn't harmful to humans - except in concentrated doses.

The polytunnel wasn't completely airtight, but the gas would be contained within the space, and shouldn't be breathed in when circulating in confined spaces. It said that on the canisters, but, of course, Mickey and Melia couldn't read that from inside.

Marks turned away, pleased with himself.

Yes, he had ordered the hit on Mickey, sending Bartoli to Mickey's apartment to finish him off. It hadn't worked. Still, this 'accident' might just do it. Two people locked in the plastic tunnel, 'unknowingly', and the chemical spray turned on, by 'mistake'. It would be most unfortunate, but things do go wrong sometimes, when dealing with poisonous chemicals.

Mr Marks would be most sympathetic when his minions told him they had found two bodies in the polytunnel.

Oh, what a shame. But what were they doing there? I mean, a man and a woman, and didn't they have a relationship?

Maybe they went in for a little 'private time', he would suggest to Gibson.

That little runt! Marks was thinking. This was just the sort of bad news the Captain wouldn't want to hear. Tough!

Dolf brought the news to Mr Marks later.

It was a nice touch. Gibson didn't know the two men had a business connection, of course. Perhaps Dolf volunteered for the task, as it would give him a chance to talk with his other boss, the one paying him money.

"They're not dead," he said dispassionately, and watched with amusement the look on Marks's face.

Marks seethed. The gas was odourless, tasteless and unnoticeable. Yes, but Melia was sensitive, in her delicate condition. When she keeled over, Mickey panicked, kicked his way through the doors and carried her out to the grass beyond.

"He summoned the helicopter," Dolf reported. It was taking Melia to hospital.

He isn't going to like you, Dolf said quietly. The paramedics said there was a chance that Melia might lose her baby. If that happened, Dolf predicted, Mickey would be less than a loose cannon and more like a guided missile.

"He'll come looking for you," he predicted. Marks looked suitable irritated, but was not afraid.

"Your good pal Mickey is going to have to start living with realities," he said obstinately.

In the first place, he told Dolf, I have been offered a seat in the House of Lords. It changes my status. I am no longer a mere honoured visitor to your shores, I am now a key member of the Establishment.

Dolf looked doubtful, but Marks was assured. Crapanza has paid enough into party funds to guarantee the loyalty of many important members of the hierarchy. I am secure, Marks said. Nobody will be able to touch me.

"Then they'll attack your company," Dolf predicted. Crapanza had busily earned itself a terrible reputation with the British public. It was the pits in the small world that was the British Isles.

"Ah, but 'Crapanza' no longer exists, my friend," Marks told him, a hint of triumph in his voice.

The chemicals and food giant had been sold to another, larger conglomerate Based in Switzerland - Sagar International.

"I have been employed by Sagar for the last three years," Marks confided. Why not? It would all come out now. Secrets were secrets no longer. Mr Marks had been drawing two salaries all that time, and nobody in Crapanza had realised a thing.

"A bit like me," Dolf said, knowing that Marks would think he meant WSB British Security and him, Mr Marks.

Marks nodded. Yes, that was about the size of it. He had been sent to Britain to finalise the deal. Some people had tried to stop him, a few in Crapanza and even a few in Sagar, the directors who didn't want anything to do with a plan to take in a poison chalice like the Crap guys. That's why Marks had been in such danger: he was being targeted from both sides.

"Go back and tell your Captain Gibson he has done a good job in keeping me alive," he told Dolf. "My compliments. However, from now on, I take no orders from him, or advice, or threats. I do what I need to do. He won't be able to stop me."

Dolf was happy to smile and affirm his intentions. He watched Marks head for the door.

He still thinks I am his man, Dolf was thinking. He believes I am his creature.

"What about the bees?" he shouted, since this seemed to be a moment for truths.

Marks stopped, turned and grinned. "Oh, Sagar knows that their insecticides are killing the bees. We could stop it, and we will, if there is legislation. If not, well then we go right on earning money. That's what my company is all about."

He turned with a flourish, exited the door and let it slam behind him.

What a showman! Dolf was thinking. And what a fake. What a liar. What a deceiver.

Luckily, he, Dolf, was one step ahead of the flamboyant ego on legs.

What Marks didn't know, and would probably never find out, was that Dolf wasn't all that he seemed either. Yes, he was drawing more than one salary, the one from WSB, the British anti-terrorism unit. And one from Crapanza, or whoever Marks now worked for and had a hand in directing. But Yes, Dolf had yet one more, a third income.

From Russia.

Marks should have realised that country's importance. They had put money into Crapanza and that gave them a CEO position, one they filled with a man called Lenkov, Marks's old boss. The problem was, of course, that he was from one band of oligarchs and it was another that had taken control of Sagar. No doubt there would be a battle for power in the coming weeks, as the new Russian elites fought between themselves for overall control.

There was no reason why anyone should find any of it shocking, of course. The Western world was being rocked by a series of health scares, from obesity to diabetes, from autism to asthma. Who would have the most to gain from illness and disability in Europe and America? Why, their enemies, of course. No wonder Russia was putting money into Genetically Modified Food, processed food, convenience food, Fast Food, and all the rest of the products that were clogging arteries and making the population ill.

It was the sweetest, most clever form of Biological Warfare that had ever been devised.

But in this case, it wasn't poison gas, like in the First World War, or defoliants, like in Vietnam. It was food, delicious food, that the local inhabitants were happy to swallow. They guzzled it up, this bio-agent, and it was killing them, relentlessly.

That's why Dolf was happy to join their side. They were the side that was going to win!

His own diet, of course, was more particular. He was careful what went into his mouth.

He wanted to live long enough to enjoy the easy life that his massive income would eventually buy him.

At the back of MacLawn's farm, Terry was out in the yard, aiming to get a signal on his private mobile phone.

He was trying to reach Liv, and didn't want to use official channels. He had news for her, about Melia.

As far as he knew, Melia was going to survive, but the gas that had got into her lungs had poisoned her blood and the life that was growing inside her was at risk. That would be a huge blow. He and Liv wanted so badly to bring up that child!

He moved out from under the orchard trees and found himself under the farm's water tower.

"Look out, below!" a voice shouted from above.

Terry looked up in alarm. It was Snopes, that Mr Snopes who claimed to be some kind of distant relative to the Snopes that Terry had worked with for many years. His Snopes was an idealistic young man whom Terry had admired and liked a lot.

This Snopes, from what he had heard, apart from being a stalker to Melia, was also an annoyance and a bully.

What was he doing? Terry realised, with a shock, that he was peeing, out into the farmyard.

"Hey, I don't want to be poisoned!" Terry yelled, offended and upset. He moved out of range.

"My urine," Snopes declared, "is probably far less danger to you than all the water in this water tower, and even the stuff that flows in the stream over there. Did you know that pee is naturally aseptic? It can cure wounds and kill bacteria."

"I'd prefer my water pure," Terry yelled back, "after it's been through the filtration system, not through you."

"Oh, yeah. 'Pure'. I hear that a lot. We don't have pure water in this country. We can't get the antibiotics out of it. Or the birth control hormones. Or any medication, come to that. We're all being medicated, with your so-called 'pure' water."

Now wait a minute, Terry was thinking, I've had this conversation.

Oh yeah, it's what Mickey told him he had learned when he went to that Water Filtration Plant in Lancashire. But someone else had told Mickey that, not this runt up the tower now. Maybe the technician there. What was his name? A man who worked for Techmark.

Or was it Jenner? That sounded more like it. Dr Jenner had had a conversation with Mickey, in a cafe called Miles, a long time ago, and said something about water, or maybe a lot of things. Allegations. Assertions. That's what had launched this whole bizarre operation. Right from the beginning, it was all about water.

"I'll give you 'pure' water," the Snopes relative sneered, and raised a bottle to his lips.

Why? What was he doing here? Was he on site to see Melia, was that his plan? He had followed her down here?

Or was there something more? He couldn't have come with Melia, she wouldn't have allowed that, a civilian in the same area as the WSB team. No, there was only one other possibility, then. He was here with the 'other side', the Crapanza lot.

Mr Snopes, the grieving relative, was yet another Crap employee. My God, how many people were they bribing!

Terry was disappointed, but not surprised. It seemed like the company had a talent for picking slobs and losers.

"Don't make me come up there!" he shouted at the idiot on the tower.

He didn't have to worry. Mr Snopes came to him.

Snopes was swigging from the bottle, but maybe it wasn't water. Maybe it was something stronger. In fact, he had been drinking all day, a sad and frustrated young man, in love with Melia, or so he thought, as many did. But unrequited.

He was one who liked a grand gesture. Seeing the tower, he had climbed it, and was walking around the thing, clinging to the railing, more or less precariously. Now, drinking, he wasn't looking where he was going.

Worse, he gulped a little too heartily, and started to cough. Then he was choking. Then he couldn't breathe.

He reached out, missed his grip and tumbled over the side. He fell ten metres onto concrete.

Terry breathed in sharply. What is it? he was thinking. Why do people keep dying around me?

His phone was buzzing.

Terry flicked it idly and a voice started talking to him.

"Terry?" Liv said. "Terry. Did you call me? What's going on? What's happening, Terry?"

Damned if I know, Terry was thinking.

THE END

About the Author

What can you say about Mike Scantlebury - that hasn't been said a thousand times, and with a lot more venom?

Try this.

He was born in Alaska but moved to England when quite young. His family settled in the West Country, near a town called Cullompton, where his father took a job on the iron road. When the riding of rails became less attractive after Beeching, Mike packed a travelling bag and moved into a flat with some young friends in the big city of Bristol. This is where he first got involved in appearing in folk clubs, wrote songs, and became interested in all forms of massage.

You can find Mike Scantlebury on the internet.

But don't try looking for 'Mike Scantlebury: books' because there's another author – same name, different books. Not crime fiction, not thrillers. (But also from Canada.)

BOTH Mikes are on Amazon and Kindle.

Here's Mike's Author Page on Amazon:
http://www.amazon.co.uk/Mike-Scantlebury/e/B0088IX1J8/

It's @MikeScantlebury on Twitter and 'mikescantlebury99' on Facebook. And, surprise, 'mikescantlebury' on Linked In.

If you want to see Mike singing and posing, try Youtube.
https://www.youtube.com/user/mikescantlebury

If all else fails, try him at home (he's not often there): http://www.Salford.me/

Other Books by Mike Scantlebury

(author of Scanti-Noir)

The Amelia Hartliss Mystery series

Book One: Poison Doctor
Book Two: Hartliss Running
Book Three: Prince William (At Olympics 2012)
Book Four: Con-Fusion
Book Five: Mayors' Tales
Book Six: Secret Garden Festival 2012
Book Seven: Kidnapping Cameron
Book Eight: Secret Garden 2013
Book Nine: Fresh Heir
Book Ten: The Golden Chip
Book Eleven: The Folksinger 2013
Book Twelve: Salford World War
Book Fourteen: Salford Trenches
Book Fifteen: Terror Beach
Book Sixteen: A Shot at Mayor
Book Seventeen: JC's Cure for Cancer

The Mickey from Manchester series

Book One: Black and White
Book Two: Off The Rails
Book Three: A Limp Piccolo

Book Four: Filling In
Book Five: New, Clear Future
Book Six: Housing Erases Debts
Book Seven: The Bone Key Curse
Book Eight: Multimedia (*BBC comes to Salford*)
Book Nine: Lucky Ignatius
Book Ten: Reverend Dumb
Book Eleven: Jennercide
Book Twelve: Lethal Election
Book Fourteen: Trumps A Mayor
Book Fifteen: Senctioned
Book Sixteen: 75 Years